Great Fire

By Jon Chant

MOGZILLA

Great Fire

First published by Mogzilla in 2015

Paperback edition:
ISBN:978-1-906132-30-9

Printed in the UK

http://www.mogzilla.co.uk/greatfire

www.writebackintime

"For Pepe and his grandmother."

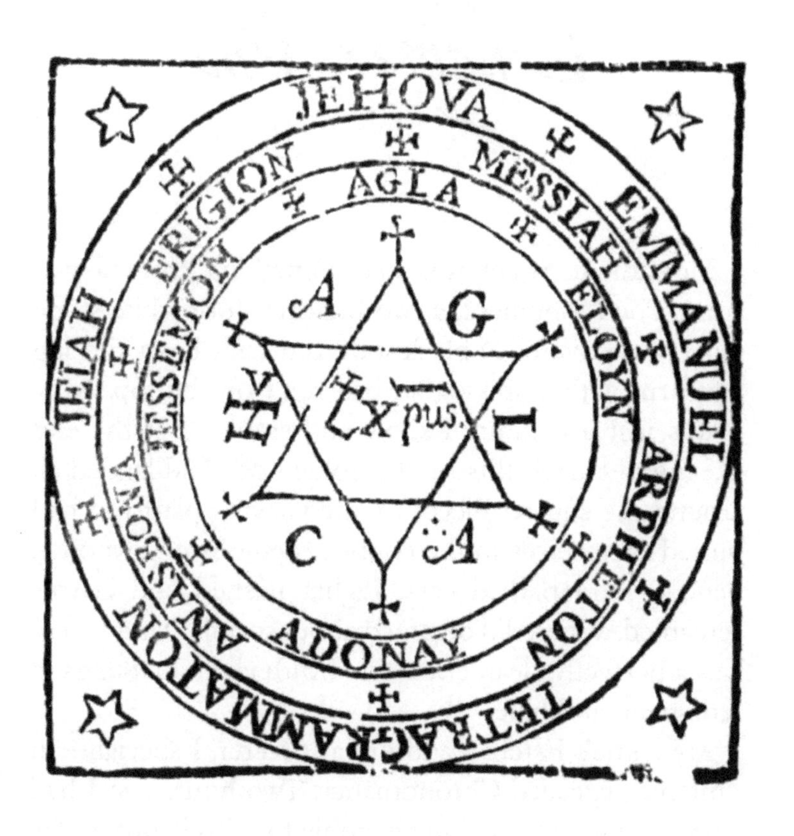
JEHOVA
EMMANUEL
ARPHETON
TETRAGRAMMATON
JEIAH
MESSIAH
ELOYN
JESSEMON
ERIGION
AGLA
ADONAY
A G L A
C H
Xpus

Chapter One

Monument Street was like something from a war zone. The Monument, a two-hundred-foot white stone pillar, was covered in black soot. It usually has a viewing platform with a spiky gold ball right on the top. Now it was just a column, hollow and smoking at the end like a gun barrel. Bits of the golden orb had landed all around the square. Pieces of the viewing platform had buried themselves in the cobbles, demolishing wooden benches and parked cars. Lights flashed and alarms screamed. Where I'd dreamed about seeing Danny there was a perfectly clean circle filled with chalk markings in red, green and blue.

My name's Esteban and I'm a sorcerer. I specialise in time magic, called Chronomancy. Two hours ago I had a dream where something horrible tore itself out of the city. It was like watching a wasp larva hatch out of a spider. I saw fire raging everywhere.

In the middle, my friend Danny was trying to hold a circle. That's what Danny does, he's a conjurer: the ones who draw magic circles and exorcise 'Things That Shouldn't Be Here'.

If the house hadn't been so powerfully warded I would probably have spent the night throwing up and clutching my head like the other magical people in London. Running, fighting, more running, getting burned. I'd have missed all that. Lucky me, eh?

The dream started just before midnight. Everyone has weird dreams, but when you're time sensitive you learn to tell the difference between weird and magic. Some people see totem animals, I hear music: I call it the Devil's ringtone.

There were no people outside, no night busses. A car went around and around the roundabout at Elephant and Castle. I managed to catch a glimpse of the driver's face as he got to the turning for London Road, forgot what he was doing and went around again.

Certain things are the magical equivalent of seeing a mushroom cloud over the city. London was beginning to close itself off to non-magical people.

I hurried, following the landmarks from my dream. I knew where I was going: the Monument. The City's two-hundred foot memorial to the Great Fire of London. At the top of Borough High Street the buildings dropped away. Orange street lights reflected off a cloud of smoke that was seeping out from behind some riverside offices.

I smelled wood and paper smoke on the breeze. I swear I heard the Devil's ringtone somewhere under the blaring alarms – burglar alarms, fire alarms, car alarms. I dashed out onto the bridge, black water flowing fast underneath me.

A ragged homeless man appeared out of nowhere. He had long, dirty hair and an eye patch. I bumped into him, bouncing off.

"Sorry," I muttered, looking him up and down.

"Umm…"

"Mother London's gathering her children," he said. He peered at me with his good eye. "Go back to bed, boy."

"Yeah…"

I walked faster, breaking into a run.

The screaming of a dozen different alarms hammered at my skull. Pieces of stone and brass appeared to be embedded in solid concrete.

"Who...?"

It was a girl's voice. She sounded about my age, posh and northern, with a voice like a well educated fog-horn.

"Who are you?" she said. "Sorry, that sounds weird but there are some weird things going on."

If my head hadn't been so full of shock and magic, I would have seen her immediately. There was no way she'd blend in with a crowd. She was five foot eleven in flat shoes, with skin so pale it almost glowed. Her hair was bright white and she wore huge, round dark glasses. At night.

"How did you get in? You're the first person I've seen," she said holding out her phone. "I can't get any reception."

She didn't feel magical, but the whole place buzzed with fading power.

"How long have you been here?" I asked.

I tried to concentrate but the screaming alarms wouldn't let me.

"I… I was out of it for a while," she frowned. "I couldn't get any phone reception so I walked up the hill, but even when I got through to the police they kept hanging up on me."

"And then you came back here?" I looked at her properly: she was dressed to go out. She was wearing a pink shirt and a black overcoat. Her hair was bright, brilliant white.

"What can I do?" she asked. "I can't just walk off and leave. I was hoping to find a policeman. I thought someone would have come to the explosion by now… but there's just you. Look, who are you?"

"It would sound a bit mad if I tried to explain," I said. "Did you see a mixed race guy with dreadlocks? About your height, with a brimmed hat?" I asked.

"That's my other half," she replied. "So who are you?"

"I'm Esteban," I replied. "Danny's a close friend of mine too. I think he's in trouble."

The dark glasses made it hard to read her expression, but I could feel the oncoming violence.

She grabbed my coat and pulled me up so hard I stood on tiptoes. I managed to break her grip and step away.

"He's never mentioned a girlfriend to me," I said.

The pale girl pushed her dark glasses up and gave me a smile full of teeth.

"Funnily enough he never mentioned a fat, curly-haired midget to me," she said.

It hurt, but it's a fair description.

"Yeah? Tell me something only a close friend would know," I said.

"Alright," She tilted her head to one side, "How about, 'Within the Oracle Spirits of the city, the four elements are not fully represented. Earth is represented by The Knowledge. Water is represented by Themsus and Air is represented twice by The Shard and The Old Lady of Threadneedle Street. Within that scheme the fact that the element of Fire is missing stands out most incongruously…'"

"That sounds like Taylor's Spirits of London," I said. "Danny started reading it last week."

The girl sat back against a traffic bollard, putting her face in her hands.

"Blooded nails!" her voice shook. "Where are the police? Where are the people?"

"It's the City of London at night," I lied. "No one's around at the weekends."

"But where are the constables? I must have been here an hour. We've been hit by a massive explosion. You'd think people would notice."

"Honestly?" I asked. "No exaggerating?"

"Well..."

She looked up, her eyes still hidden by the shades. "There was a one-eyed tramp…"

"Yeah," I said. "I saw him."

I closed my eyes and reached out through time.

Being a conjurer, Danny does creatures: things that shouldn't be here and don't properly exist in our world. 'Traditional' magicians call it the highest art. They look at what I do like a physicist looks at a world donut eating champion.

I reached out and took the alarms back to a time before they'd been triggered. It didn't take much: they stopped all at once. Or at least, they should have.

An air-raid siren moaned through the dark.

I crossed myself. "Hostia…"

I had a sudden sinking feeling. If the girl hadn't been there…

"That's why no one came," I tried to keep my voice

calm. "Can you hear it?"

The girl frowned, straining to hear. "It's… yes…" she said. "It's like a siren?"

"It is." I nodded. "Normal people can't hear that at all. It just makes them want to forget about the area and stay away from it. The fact that you're still here suggests you've got power."

"Power?" The girl crossed her arms. "Are you a nutcase?"

"Hasn't anything strange ever happened to you? Or you've seen something no one else can see? Maybe someone said something in a strange voice, and everyone else believed it but you?" I asked.

"This is just rubbish," said the girl, shaking her head. "It's just a siren, probably because of the explosion. I'm not going to listen to this."

"Good answer." I nodded. "Go home. I'm better off without you."

I started walking towards the Monument, leaving footprints in the soot.

"Go home?" She followed me. "I'm not going home, I'm going to find someone who can help."

"Look," I turned. "I don't know what happened and I don't have a plan, but this is really bad, and I'm really sorry, but there is no-one to help. Maybe me, but probably not. I'm probably just here to look for Danny and go home."

"But it's not possible…" she said uncertainly.

"Okay," I said brightly. "Fair enough. Go and find the police."

I turned again, and started walking.

"Look… we've got to do something," she said.

"Surely… we can't be literally on our own?"

"We are. That's the rule: you hear about something, or if it falls into your lap, you go and sort it out. There isn't any ministry of magic. There's just people. I had a dream this would happen, so I'm here. If I'd seen anyone else on my way I would have gone back to bed, but I didn't."

"You saw the tramp," she said.

"Yeah, and he was off in the opposite direction as fast as he could go," I replied.

"Then why don't we see dragons on the news, or monsters with tentacles swallowing cities?" she asked.

"Have you ever heard of Redchester? Or Bridlingforth?" I asked. "They were the second and third largest cities in England."

She looked at me suspiciously, "I might have. I don't know why, though. It sounds like you just made them up."

"They're gone, and all we could do was seal the wound – like with Atlantis and Leng," I said. "That's all we can do when things go really wrong."

"Is that what's happening here?" She adjusted her dark glasses. "Things are going really wrong?"

"Might be." I said.

"Then I'm not letting you sort it out on your own," she said.

"Yeah, alright." I sighed. "What happened with you and Danny?"

"We've been going out for a couple of weeks," she said. "I'm really into history, so we've been talking about the Great Fire of London. We came here on Saturday to climb to the top of…"

She shrugged as she looked at the empty space at the top of the Monument where the viewing platform had once stood.

"And last night Danny asked me to meet him here at midnight."

"What was he doing when you arrived?" I asked.

"He was kneeling on the ground, inside the circle. I was quite freaked out," she said. "He was doing the whole thing: magic words and prayers. He had a stick of incense but I don't think it survived the fire."

"That's a surprise," I said.

She waved a hand. "Anyway, I think I might be the reason it all went wrong."

I gave her a quizzical look.

"I didn't know what was going on. I stood there while he shouted nonsense and then fire started coming out of the top of the Monument," she explained.

"What did you do?" I asked.

"I might have had a bit of a scream."

She glowered at me. "Look, what would you have done? You'd have screamed your head off. Anyway, that wasn't the problem. I panicked, I thought the Monument was going to fall on him."

"What did you do then?"

She looked at her feet. "I jumped into the circle. I was going to barge him out of the way," she said.

I looked up at the smoking wreck of the Monument. Apart from the soot, the pillar didn't look too badly damaged.

"No," I said. "That wouldn't have done this. It must have been right on the edge of falling anyway. It probably would have gone up tonight whether or not you'd have been here."

I looked at her again. I could feel the magical energy crackling inside her now.

"He might have been trying to sort it out," I said. "Look, don't take this the wrong way but he might have been planning on using you as a battery."

"That's flattering."

She tucked a strand of hair behind her ear.

"Sorry," I said. "Anyway, I don't think he would have been your boyfriend just for energy." Flakes of soot settled like snow. "What happened after that?"

"The explosion. I must have been out of it for a bit," she said. "When I came to, Danny was gone."

She hesitated. "I think he's alive. There would be bits of him still here if he wasn't… I mean…"

"Urgh, that's grim."

I looked around the square. "It's true, though. There would have been pieces and the circle wouldn't have stayed clear."

"So…" she stuck her hand out to be shaken. "I'm Connie."

I shook the hand. "I'm Esteban." I looked at the circle. "I don't really know what Danny was trying to do. It looks like he was trying to see the Monument astrally, to understand if it had any magic."

"Is that dangerous?" she asked.

"It shouldn't have been. He would have shown you whatever was inside and put the wards back up."

I looked at the two-hundred foot blasted column.

"Something huge must have been trapped there, and it must have been on a knife edge."

"What was it?" she asked. "Inside the Monument, I

mean."

"Well..." I thought for a minute. "This is the Monument, built to commemorate the Great Fire of London. There are plenty of big bad fire spirits people would want locked up."

"What does that tell us?" Connie looked around for a perch.

"Not a lot. The only way is if I look back at what was put here, then we might be able to work out what it is. Possibly what it's done with Danny."

Connie made a sceptical noise, but I ignored her. It was easy to reach back in time, pierce the veil of reality and see the power that had once been in the Monument.

At some point I started screaming.

Chapter Two

Fire. Lots of fire: roaring and chewing its way through the city. It was alive, angry and hungry. People ran away from it, tricked it and starved it. They dragged it under a machine made of buildings and city streets, all grinding magical energy into the Monument. Now it was free and bitter.

"Happy Birthday to me," Connie said.

Those were the first words I heard when I woke up. My head was resting on a rolled up coat. The fact that I could see Connie's pink shirt suggested it was hers.

"What's going on?" I struggled upright.

For a split second I thought it had been a dream. Then I realised I was lying on the pavement next to a two-hundred-foot pillar. The wailing of the air raid sirens gave me a cold shower of apprehension.

"You started screaming like a girl and fainted," Connie said. "It was something about fire, unsurprisingly."

"Okay… you actually are a girl," I said. "Are you allowed to use that as an insult?"

"I scream like a woman." Connie flicked her hair. "You scream like a girl."

She paused for consideration. "And you faint like a sack of potatoes. I had to drag you out. Your clothes are filthy."

"Hostia. My grandmother is going to kill me," I moaned.

"Isn't she a magical person, too?" Connie frowned.

"My grandmother is THE magical person," I explained as I massaged my temples. "She's the Archmage of Chronomancy, that's time magic. You only get to keep that title until someone comes along and proves they're more powerful than you. She's had it since the eighties."

Connie laughed. It was a strong laugh, the sort of laugh that rode horses and played hockey.

"What made you go all hysterical, anyway?"

"Something nasty has escaped," I said. "They locked it under this pillar. I don't know what Danny was doing, but someone has built a massive magical machine centred around the Monument."

She raised an eyebrow. "What are we going to do?"

"Hopefully we can get a look at the mechanism," I said. "Let's go around past Fisher's Hill."

We looped down onto Thames Street. London Bridge arched above us, blotting out the stars with bright orange streetlights. It usually smelled of car exhaust and petrol down here, like a garage. Tonight the air was thick with burning tar and gunpowder.

The weird thing about Thames Street is that two streets meet in the middle, right under the bridge. Someone put the two street signs next to each other, one reading 'Upper Thames Street,' the other one reading 'Lower Thames Street.'

But here's the thing: there's another street. Not everyone can find it, but if you've got the talent and a little bit of training, you'll know it's there. You'll feel it, like a word on the tip of your tongue.

"There," I pointed. "That's where we need to be."

"Where? What did you see?" Connie hung back.

I stopped and peered at the concrete wall, looking for a specific spot. "Sorry about this, I'm not trying to string you along, it's just really hard to get tonight."

"What is?" Connie gave the wall an exasperated look.

I wish I could have triumphantly said, 'This!' and opened the portal. But life never works that way. Instead it took another five minutes of staring and poking. Connie watched, increasingly suspiciously, with her arms crossed.

It didn't matter: I found it.

There was a hairline crack in reality, running dead centre between the signs. Middle Thames Street appeared as if it had always been there. Connie jumped.

"Sorcery," Connie whispered, staring.

"Well... yeah." I said. "Basically."

It wasn't hard to spot that there was something weird going on: like the fact that the street should have been a tunnel under the Monument, but it had open sky above it. It was dark like a city without streetlights. The houses were made of earth and wood with uneven paths instead of tarmac.

"Pudding Lane." Connie said. "Where the Great Fire of London started."

"Middle Thames Street," I said. "I've never been here before, it's supposed to be private property. Hopefully they won't mind."

"Is this something to do with your 'vision?'" she asked.

"Nice of you not to say 'freakout.'" I said. "And yeah,

we're under the Monument now – theoretically."

"Is this a replica of Pudding Lane?" she asked. "It's perfect: that building is Farryner's Royal Bakehouse, where the Great Fire of London started."

"Yeah… I think that's where we're going," I said.

"You'll notice that I haven't said either of us is going mad," Connie said. "But I'm getting really sick of not understanding what's going on."

"Alright." I raised my hands apologetically. "If that bakery was where the fire started, then magically speaking it's the centre of the fire: in space, time and on the Astral plane. That means they built their own bakery to be the prison for whatever was kept here. Probably."

We stopped outside the front door. It was wooden, with an iron ring handle. There was probably a bolt on the other side, which would hopefully be unlocked.

"What do you think it is?"

Connie looked at me; her huge dark lenses reflected the moonlight. Actually, everything about her glowed in the moonlight. In fact, she just glowed. I'm not being romantic, either. It was slightly disturbing. I made a mental note to ask how she could see anything with shades at night.

"Okay," I said. "So you know that they never found out exactly what caused the fire? They found out it started in this building, but–"

"The wood in Thomas Farryner's oven was found safe and unburned after the fire died out," Connie interrupted. "The brick oven had protected it. They never found out what made the building catch fire."

"What if this was just the touchdown for something unnatural?" I said. "The Great Fire could have been a living thing."

Connie grimaced. "And Danny was trying to do… something… with it on my birthday," she said. "Wonderful. Happy Birthday."

"Cut him a bit of slack," I said. "Birthdays are powerful times, he was probably thinking that you would be at your most powerful against whatever gigantic fiery monster was kept here."

"Well he'd be wrong," she said. "I'm really scared of fire. He knew that."

"Oh," I said. "Sorry."

Connie shook her head. "I'm more scared of fire than anything," she hissed. "I don't even like looking at it as a moving picture."

"What?" I asked, pulling at the bakery door.

"TV," she said. "I don't even like watching fires on TV."

"Really?" I said. "It's a bit of weird for you to be so interested in the Great Fire of London."

"It's a therapy thing," she said.

There wasn't much I could say to that. I flexed time and opened the door. Inside was dimly lit with dribbling, misshapen candles. The smell hit me like a brick wall.

"That's rank."

I coughed into my sleeve. "What is that smell?"

"Pork tallow." Connie stepped into the dimness. "It's a sort of liquified fat that was used to make candles. It's cheaper than bee's wax."

"Oh." I tried not to breath. "That's foul!"

Connie shook her head. "You're such a baby."

"I'm going vegetarian," I said.

My eyes were getting used to the smoke and the

darkness. Inside, the bakery was almost hollow. The entire ground floor was a single room with nothing but a sea of candles surrounding elaborately-drawn circles.

"Magic circles?" said Connie, looking around. "And little model buildings… what for?"

Most of the circles were black with soot, their candles burned out.

"I don't know…" I said. "But I'd guess they represent all the places the Great Fire burned down."

"Maybe," said Connie peering at the circles. "Yes, that looks like the Royal Exchange, and that could be the old St. Pauls… Oh, and there's the Guild Hall."

There was only one circle still intact: a circle of candle light around a china model of Farryner's Royal Bake House.

"It's still contained," I said, pointing to the model. "The circle around this building hasn't burned out yet."

Connie looked. She reached into her pocket for a perfume bottle and dabbed a bit of it onto her wrists. The floral scent covered up the smell of pork tallow.

"That's better," I said. "What kind of perfume is that?"

Connie waved away my comment.

"Is that the core of the spell?" she asked. "I can't believe they kept something so powerful trapped with candle spells and magic circles."

"You could keep it tied up with a strongly worded email if you had enough power," I said. "And the whole of London was rebuilt as a magical machine. They couldn't do as much as they wanted, but they still made a network of buildings and streets that shove magical energy directly into this room. That's a pretty advanced question about magic, by the w–"

There was a breeze and we both felt something snap. The candles started going out.

"That wasn't me!"

Connie jumped back. "I didn't do that."

"It was so weak, just looking at it broke the magical field," I said, turning. "Get out!"

Darkness shot around the circle of lights, starting on the southernmost point and spreading around both sides. A final spot of light held out for two heartbeats and guttered into disgusting, greasy smoke.

Something horrible broke loose from the Astral plane and slid into the room. I felt an unpleasant shifting in the air and from Connie's expression I could see that she could feel it too.

A figure appeared in the centre of the circle, a hideous thing standing on two legs. It had the tail of a wolf with the body of a goat, and its head looked like a giant tumour with ears. Claws and ridged goat horns glistened nastily in the dark. Goat eyes stared malevolently out of a face on its chest.

"What is that thing?" I asked.

I backed towards the door; I hadn't really expected an answer, but Connie surprised me.

"It's a Portent. It was born up the road on Cornhill. They wrote about it in the almanacs," she said, her voice on the edge between hysteria and panic. "But it was from before the fi–"

The creature burst into flames. Waves of fire shot around the room. Connie shrieked and covered her face. By the time I realised what was happening the door and the wall were already alight. Connie screamed.

Chapter Three

Flames raged all around us. The door and the entire front wall were blazing fiercely.

The only way to go was upstairs.

"This way."

I grabbed Connie's hand and dragged her past the flames and I ran. Connie managed a stumbling jog, clamping her shades to her face and keeping a death grip on my hand.

"The stairs!" she yelled.

The goat-thing shot a plume of flame towards us. It must have been weak from captivity, because we outran it, clambering up the wooden stairs into a square room.

"Here!" Connie ran to the window.

There was no glass, just wooden shutters. She kicked them wide open.

"There's a ledge," she yelled. "Come on, quickly."

Connie was already out the window by the time I'd crossed the room. I'm not great with heights but I'm less great with dying, so I edged out onto the six-inch wooden beam, clinging on for dear life. Inside the bakery, fire chewed through the building.

The wall was hot, and I couldn't stop thinking of how far the street was below me. My heart pounded.

The goat thing roared. Fire burst out of the window.

"Come on!"

Connie dragged me back inside and down more steps. In the bakery, the thing roared again. We fumbled with the door and burst out onto the street.

"Oh, this is bad," I said. "Hands up who feels like they just doomed the city?"

"I hate fire," said Connie trembling. She was even paler than before, if that was possible.

"You saved us," I said.

"Oh god, I hate fire…" Connie let out a shuddering breath. "What are we going to do?" she asked, burying her face in her hands.

"Come on," I said awkwardly, patting her shoulder.

"We have to stop it!" she screamed. She looked up, still wearing her dark glasses. "Nothing scares me like that." She balled her fists. "Nothing."

Magic surged around us. Figures appeared in the darkness.

Connie stared at them. They formed a bucket chain, throwing water onto the burning houses. Figures with huge, hook-ended poles stood by as a man with a massive curly wig chewed his knuckle.

"If Danny's okay he'll be trying to cast a circle," I said. "We should try and find him. Together, we might be able to stop this."

"That's…" Connie whispered. She stared at the man in the wig. "Is that…?"

"It would be Sir Thomas Bloodworth," I said. "We have to go. He doesn't try to stop the fire, he goes back to bed instead. The rest of the city's defences will be activating. I can think of one place where Danny might have gone."

A man with a powdered wig and an eye patch whispered into Bloodworth's ear. Bloodworth – a big, barrel chested man with dark curly hair – put on a show of laughing heartily.

"Fie, Valentine!" he said. "Tis nothing."

I couldn't read Connie's expression properly because of the dark glasses, but I could see that she was still trembling. Her teeth clamped together so hard that they squeaked.

"Connie," I said. "We've got to go now, come on!"

"You! You're Sir Thomas Bloodworth, Mayor of London."

Connie dashed towards Bloodworth. Bloodworth didn't hear her. He nodded towards the one-eyed man.

"Report to the King, Captain Knight," said the Mayor. "A woman could pish this fire out."

Connie hit the Mayor, hammering her fists on his chest.

"You have to stop it!" she shouted. "Cut the ships loose from the docks, at least!"

Mayor Bloodworth hardly seemed to notice her. He yawned and patted his mouth.

"Certainly it is not as grave as the '57 fire. I doubt supplies will be disrupted," said Mayor Bloodworth.

The one-eyed man smiled, nodding.

"Of course. I shall say as much to the King. A woman could pish it out. Most amusing," he said.

"Fie. It might have called me from my sleep, but now I shall return to my bed," said the Mayor.

"You idiot!" Connie shouted, hitting him again.

"He's a shade," I explained, pulling her away. "He can

barely sense you exist."

"He's an idiot," Connie spat.

"They don't know we're here," I said. "We can't change anything."

Connie shook her head and let me guide her away from the fire.

I didn't notice it at the time, but the one-eyed man watched us go.

Chapter Four

We jogged up the hill and through the maze of streets at the top of London Bridge. A huge, old department store looked down cheerfully. Part of me wished I could see The Shard, with its red eye watching the city. I don't know why, but I've always liked new buildings.

There was a 'whump' and a tongue of flame blossomed into the air. Connie flinched.

"Bloodworth didn't hold the fire," I said. "The defences aren't going to work."

"Is it the Great Fire?" she asked. "The thing under the Monument? It felt the same."

I nodded.

"It won't get far," Connie watched the firelight. "All the buildings are made of stone."

"Some of them are," I said, leading her down a side street. "But even the ones that are made of brick have timber frames, plus the insides of most modern buildings are basically paper."

"Really?" Connie looked disgusted. "Wonderful, I love progress. Where are we going?"

We were on Cannon street, which was the start of a highway that eventually went all the way down to Buckingham Palace. A roar erupted behind us. We walked quickly, then jogged. Cannon Street Station, a huge glass-and-metal railway station, stood opposite a two thousand year old lump of masonry called 'The London Stone.' Something unpleasant twisted behind me.

"Did you feel that?" said Connie, breaking into a run.

"Yeah," I said. "I think it's the Great Fire."

"What does it want?" Connie asked.

I shook my head.

"I don't know. I don't know what it wanted the first time. If we did, we might be able to work out a way to stop it without hurting anyone."

Connie stumbled, fished her phone out of her pocket and tried ringing Danny. Nothing happened.

"Nothing," she said. "Have you got one?"

"Advanced electronics and magic don't mix," I said. "What doesn't get smashed by things from beyond the walls of reality gets ruined by time magic. For all we know Danny's phone is powder."

Connie raised an eyebrow.

"Alright."

I got my phone out. "But it's low on credit and it's really old."

Connie was about to try calling Danny when there was a roar of flames at the top of the street. Fire appeared over the crest of a shimmering wave.

"I don't understand," Connie said. "It can't be this fast!"

I heard the Devil's ringtone, the sound that my time sensitivity makes just before something magical tries to destroy me. It chimed over everything else, cutting through the night like the world's most annoying doorbell.

The fire was coming down the street. It wasn't as fast as us, but it was gathering speed. A wave of change rippled ahead of it: stone walls turned to wood and pitch, and roofs turned from modern materials to wooden beams and slate. That tune, the Devil's ringtone, played in the back of my head as I felt the distinctive sensation of chronomancy. I watched a posh restaurant turn into a wooden shop, instantly consumed by the flames. The Portent, the goat-wolf-nightmare, pranced in front of it.

"It has time magic." I said. "Oh, this is bad…"

I reached through time and threw obstacles in its path: men with hooked poles tore down burning houses; brass fire-engines squirted water at the blaze. It was as effective as throwing chairs in front of a steamroller.

"Esteban," Connie said. "I think we can safely say that if it didn't work then, it won't work now."

A powerful, burning hot wind had started up, carrying sparks and burning cinders that died as they drifted too far from the time distortion.

"We can't stay here. We're going to Baynard's Castle," I said. "They're the narrow streets west of Farringdon Road. If we get separated, go to Middle Temple. I'll try to meet you there."

Connie looked at me, my own face was reflected in her dark glasses as she nodded. There was a deafening roar from the centre of the fire.

"Oh–" I said.

The Portent howled and capered. It charged, fire surging after it with a whoosh of combustion.

"No," Connie whimpered. "Blooded nails! No!"

"Connie," I said, sounding calmer than I felt. "Hold

on. We'll both be destroyed if you panic."

Connie nodded, her distant expression coming back to normal.

"This way!" she dragged me down a side street.

"They're too narrow, it'll cut us off."

I looked back. As if to prove my point, fire blossomed in front of us, rushing towards us from both sides. Unbearably hot wind and choking smoke filled the air. We threw ourselves to the floor and the fire leapt over our heads, almost hitting the Portent, which danced out of the way.

Flickering shapes stopped here and there to show a ghostly arm or a split-second outline.

"What are those things?" Connie scrabbled to her feet, running through a car park into another street.

"Echoes of the people," I shouted. "If the time shift gets any more powerful, they'll become more real."

We ran through the car park that turned into a narrow street of wooden houses. The two walls of fire met in the middle, then joined and followed us with the goat-wolf still dancing and capering in front. More figures flickered around us, flitting about faster than our eyes could follow.

"They're the people of London," I said. "It's speeding time up. For them the fire is still taking days."

We ran. The street opened up ahead, revealing a church and a park. Water trickled in a fountain that soon wouldn't be there. We ran as hard as we could, but the rows of timber-framed houses sprang up around us and the fire raced along them. The orange of the street lights faded away, leaving only firelight.

Suddenly a gap yawned open in the black outlines of

the wooden houses.

"We must be near Garlickhythe," Connie said. "Which is both good… and bad," she gasped.

Wooshing, crackling fire and shattering timbers chased along behind us. I reached through time, seeing spots from the effort. Wooden houses collapsed. Feeble jets of water hissed in the path of the flames.

So close to the river, the flickering bucket chains could attack the fire, but it wasn't going to be enough. I conjured an Elizabethan fire engine – all brass water-tanks and hand pumps – but they hadn't invented the hose yet. I watched the fire engine's fixed nozzle spit pathetic streams of water. This was one of the lost engines: by the time the fire got close the crew would have to abandon it to avoid getting burned.

"This is ridiculous," Connie said, pulling me away from where I was trying to hold the fire. "Can't you just summon a storm, or one of the fire engines from the blitz?"

"Yeah, absolutely," I said, letting the 17th century fire engine fade into the past. "Just like you can probably sing twinkle twinkle little star backwards hopping on one leg."

The fire bellowed, surging forward. We ran, skidding around a hairpin corner, half falling down the steep hill. I cast around to see the goat-wolf but there was no sign of it.

"Blooded nails! It's all burning," said Connie.

"We're going to be alright." I said, grabbing her hand.

We'd come out into Garlickhythe. For the moment it was just a few benches in front of a church. The darkness picked out the shape of a statue: a man herding turkeys.

"What?" Connie stopped to get her breath, staring at the statue.

The shimmering wave of old London caught up with us: the road vanished and the church changed. The flagstones and benches became a wooden jetty. Baskets and barrels stood out ready to be loaded onto dark ships that bobbed on the water; barrels stood full of gunpowder ready to be sent to the navy. The road beyond became the river, full of ships. The sort of ships that carried gunpowder.

"Why have they packed the place full of warships and explosives?"

I looked at Connie, her white hair glowing in the moonlight.

"We were at war," Connie said. "This is gunpowder for the fleet."

"Oh no," I said. "Run!"

We were moving, but I'm not used to running so far. The fire was already creeping over the roof of St. James', Garlickhythe. Once it reached the dock the gunpowder would go off like a bomb, as would the ships.

"Up the hill," I panted. "And then around past St. Paul's."

I thought I saw someone moving. It was a good excuse to stop for breath.

"What was that?" I asked Connie.

"I can't see." Connie paused unwillingly. It might have helped if she'd taken her dark glasses off. "Where?" she demanded.

"I saw something," I said. "In the shadows over there."

I pointed to the darkness and smoke next to the

burning church. Connie peered through the darkness. She was about to say something when, far away, there was an explosion. I froze in my tracks, staring at the barrels right next to us.

"It's Limehouse," Connie said, grabbing my hand. "About now in 1666, sailors were using gunpowder to fight the fire. We're alright! Come on."

The fire swept down as the church's roof crashed inwards. Scraps of burning wood and red-hot stone rained down on the wooden jetty. I ran, wishing I'd spent more time outside enjoying healthy exercise.

I've never run up such a steep slope. In fact I'd probably done more running in the last few minutes than I'd done in the last year. By the time we got to the top I could barely move.

"Why… hasn't it… gone off?" I gasped.

The Portent made a sound like hyenas and mad crows. The firelight framed it at the bottom of the hill but I couldn't make myself move. Even if I was prepared to throw up, there was no way I was going to move. My life had had too much good food and TV to survive this.

"Leave me," I staggered a few steps. "Get to where I said. There might be someone who can help. If not, get far away."

"No..."

Connie rummaged through her pockets.

The fire converged on the Portent. It started charging up the hill towards us.

"Go!" I said.

I could see the loose mouth and slit eyes in its chest, and the way its tumour-head flopped around as it ran. Horns and claws and hooves shone in the firelight.

I tried to run a few steps. If Connie thought I was running, maybe she'd run too.

"Go, it's alright," I said. "Go!"

Connie shook her head silently, glancing up at the Portent as she patted herself down. I managed another few feet and collapsed with my lungs burning. I couldn't run any more. Not even to save Connie's life.

Hot air whirled around me. Firelight burned brightly. Something dropped out of Connie's pocket, rolling down the hill. Her eyes widened.

"Esteban!" she yelled. "Get out of the way!"

I hauled myself a few feet forward as a glass bauble rolled down the hill, between the goat-wolf's legs, and vanished into the fire.

I looked up at Connie just as it exploded. Snow and ice-cold water picked me up and threw me forward, tumbling me head over heels up the hill. The Portent howled in pain. The fire was whooshing and hissing with indignation. It looked between us and what was left of the Great Fire.

"We're getting a chance," Connie said. "Let's use it."

She yanked at my arm but I didn't move.

"What was that?" I asked

"Danny gave it to me," Connie said, pulling me so hard that I stumbled. "He called it A Winter's Tale."

"And you didn't think there was anything going on?" I asked.

"I thought it was a Christmas decoration," Connie said.

I started moving. My legs didn't feel like they were going to carry me much further. We were at the top of the hill when Garlickhythe exploded.

Chapter Five

As the smoke cleared we realised we weren't alone. A figure stood over us.

"Blessed Virgin! what have you done to your clothes?" she asked.

It was my grandmother. 'Abuela' as I call her in Spanish. My stomach churned, and not just because of the hell she was going to give me.

I really hadn't wanted to get my grandmother involved in this. She's one of the most powerful Chronomancers on the scene at the moment, an Archmage.

The problem is, that when we get powerful, we sorcerers tend to lose our perspective on human life. Even other magical people were afraid of Abuela.

She stood over us like an avenging angel: my grandmother, a tall thin woman with dark skin and curly silver hair.

"Does this mean you're here to take over?" I asked, partly trying to get her away from thinking about my filthy shirt and trousers. "Are you going to send us home and deal with everything through your greater experience and wisdom?"

"If you wish," she said. "Look at your clothes. Do you want this girl to think I send you out of the house like this? Disgusting boy. Not to mention the way you left the house – like an elephant."

"Oh come on," I said. "You can't complain about me waking you up when you weren't even there."

"Okay…" Connie looked between us. "If no one minds me asking: what's going on?"

My grandmother sniffed imperiously. She's good at that. She could make the royal family feel common.

"Well, there are no authorities, but my grandmother and a few others take care of things." I said

Connie frowned. "I thought you said there was no-one else who could help?"

"Oh no." I laughed. "Just no one who'll care about getting Danny back."

"That is very unfair, Esteban. I can still be hurt," Abuela said. "I'm a weak old woman."

She looked Connie up and down. "As for you, I'd tell you to respect your elders, but I'm not sure…"

Abuela insists that she's a vulnerable elderly women despite the fact that none of the local gangs will walk past our flat. It's best to just agree with her.

"Sorry, Abuela," I said. "I'll make sure my stuff is clean by the time I get home."

Something flashed through her eyes, but she didn't let on. I felt a horrible needle of fear.

"Look, what are you going to do?" I asked. "With this mess?"

"You're a good boy," she said. "Even if you are so taxing for a poor, defenceless old woman at the end of her life."

"Thanks," I said, starting to get embarrassed. "So what are you going to do?"

She was quiet. I don't know what she was feeling. I don't understand what goes through my grandmother's head most of the time.

"You're going to seal the city, aren't you?" I said. "You're going to lock it up in a bubble of time and forget about it."

"Something is very wrong in the City of London," Abuela said. "Wrong enough for the city to lock itself up and start crying for help."

"Danny's involved," I said.

"And so are you," Abuela said. "Stupid boy! Did it not occur to you to ask an old woman what was going on? Did you not think to stay out of what wasn't your business?"

"Well obviously not," I snapped. "Because here I am. Anyway, I've seen what you're like."

"Do as I say is not do as I do!" Abuela said. "Oh, stupid boy."

She pinched the bridge of her nose. "Your grandfather would never have done anything like this."

"No," I said. "He'd have held your coat, and you would have done it."

Abuela gave me a look of cold rage. I started to think it might be better if I didn't survive this.

"Disrespectful boy."

She looked at Connie. "Never have children. You give them your whole life and this is the thanks you get."

"Umm," Connie said quietly. "Look, pretend I don't know anything. What are you going to do?"

My grandmother looked at me challengingly, then back to Connie. "I will seal the city," Abuela said. "I am very sorry for Daniel and anyone else involved."

"And that's it?" I felt my temper rising. "Forget about Danny? Forget about anyone who might actually live in the centre of London? Forget about anyone in a car or on a bus? Just seal them up for the rest of time?"

She looked me up and down. "Do you have a better idea, since you are so full of wisdom?"

"We've been under the Monument," I said. "There was a chamber, linked to a circuit – a sort of magical machine. Danny told me about it. We might be able to get it started again. It's not like this stuff wasn't contained safely for hundreds of years."

"That sounds like the sort of thing Daniel would say," Abuela said. "I will not act to prevent you. If you are foolish enough to risk your lives in some madness... I will do my duty and prevent this outbreak from spreading. If you are still in London when I finish my work, then so be it. You would need to find the map of this 'machine made of streets', and then you would need to find not only a conjurer, but an alchemist to make the correct tinctures. I find that unlikely. Selfish boy, putting a strain like this on an old woman."

And she was gone.

Connie stared at the space my grandmother had been standing in.

"I might be wrong, but did she just say that if we can't sort this, they're just going to lock us up in a bubble of time and throw away the key?"

"Yeah, basically," I said.

"That's cold," Connie said.

We jogged back onto Cannon Street. The fire was still moving, but we'd gained some time. Cheapside was still a modern glass and metal shopping centre, which was good. Unfortunately there was still a fiery glow coming up behind it. We stood with the hot wind blowing on our clothes. It was like being in the path of a giant hair dryer. Air raid sirens wailed. No people or cars.

"We can walk now," I said gripping Connie's shoulder.

"You need to work out," Connie said. "If we survive this you might lose some weight."

We walked, getting our breath back. Well... *my* breath. Neither of us spoke. Too much of what we could talk about involved us ending up un-alive in various ways.

"How can it be spreading so quickly?" Connie asked eventually.

"You don't just have to replay time," I said. "You can fast-forward or slow it down if you're good enough."

She frowned. "How can it be that good?"

"You know how humans can be really strong, but elephants can be stronger?" I said. "It's like that. Really powerful spirits can do a lot with time."

"Do you think you can stop this?" she asked.

"There's one thing," I said. "I know where there are some plans for the machine. It was built by Sir Christopher Wren and Robert Hook. They were scientists and architects who rebuilt London after the fire."

Connie smiled humourlessly. "This doesn't feel very scientific."

"The definition of science was a bit broader back then," I said. "There's a laboratory, left from the time of King Charles II. A lot of important magical stuff is kept there. We should be able to get into it."

"Okay, and afterwards we find Danny," Connie said. "And kick his liver until he tells us what's going on."

"*If* he knows, which he probably will. He was there when the thing broke out and he knows more about technical magic than me."

I stuck my hands in my pockets.

"Yes," Connie said. "With God's grace."

"You've got a weird accent, you know that?" I said. "Where are you from? It sounds like a mixture of Welsh, Cornish and Yorkshire. I've never heard anything like it."

Connie laughed and walked on.

The fire was getting closer as we made our way past St. Pauls. Ludgate Hill was a former riverbank, leading down to Farringdon Road. Farringdon Road was a busy, grimy highway that went under the gothic Holborn Viaduct and between various other former riverbanks. It had once been the river Fleet, until the Victorians had put twenty feet of concrete on top of it.

This far away, the Great Fire was straining to affect anything. Buildings from 1666 tried to coexist with ones from the modern day. If you looked one way it was a huge glass office building, another and it was the crumbling Fleet Prison.

Up on the hill behind us, St. Paul's Cathedral shimmered and changed. The smooth white walls turned dark yellow. High, narrow windows appeared out of the stone. Yellow stone arches reached up to support the main roof. Wooden scaffolding and grey cloth covered the walls, flapping wildly where it had been pried loose by the burning hot wind.

"The pavement's getting hot." Connie said. "Can we hurry up?"

My boots were fairly thick but Connie's shoes looked

like they were made of cardboard.

"We'd better get onto the other side of Farringdon Road before it turns into a river."

I tried to ignore how fast this was getting out of hand. We hurried down to the bottom of the slope. Time distorted and I suddenly felt as if my feet should be wet. When I stepped onto Fleet Street I even shook them as if I'd been wading.

"Can you hear that?" Connie asked.

The air was perfectly quiet and still. Compared to the burning hot winds, the normal summer night felt icy.

I strained to listen. "I can't hear anything."

"Exactly," Connie said. "No sirens, no sound of the fire…" she looked back up Ludgate Hill. "In fact, there's no sign of anything."

Looking back, Ludgate Hill was ordinary, empty and peaceful. Ordinary street lights painted it in shades of black and orange. Modern glass and metal buildings were shoulder to shoulder with stumpy Victorian offices. The station stood on one corner, a bank on the other. Traffic whispered somewhere in the distance.

"Defences of the City of London," I said. "If you didn't have some power you'd be standing here trying to work out why you were out so late."

Chapter Six

It was quite a walk up Fleet Street and through Covent Garden. London's West End is never really quiet. Even if the pubs are closed, the offices are dark and the theatres have kicked everyone out, the West End never sleeps.

We passed homeless people, awake and chatting in shop doorways. Men were carrying boxes through the side door of a restaurant. One of the theatres had its stage door open with lighting technicians drinking coffee; people waited for night busses and lost tourists looked for their hotels. After the deserted streets of the old city it felt really strange and crowded. A familiar face appeared in the crowd.

"Go home, boy," the one-eyed man said. "You're out of your depth."

"Who are you?" I demanded.

The one-eyed man looked at us and spat on the floor. He was taller than me, but stick thin.

I lunged for him. He grabbed me by the hair and threw me to the floor. Connie barked something incomprehensible and tried to kick him in the shins. It didn't connect.

"You should have slipped off into the darkness," he

hissed. "Some people don't have any dignity."

"What do you know about this?" I asked as I clambered to my feet. "What did you do?"

"I didn't do nothing," the one-eyed man laughed. "You kids should learn proper history."

He didn't need to tell me anything. If I could get hold of him, I could look back through his time stream.

The one-eyed man looked at Connie. He smiled, his teeth rotten. "Take him home," he said. "It'll soon be over."

Connie fixed him with an angry look.

"We'll stop you, she said. "Whatever you're doing."

I lunged for him again. He kicked me in the stomach, sending me rolling away.

"You'll run around from here to there," he said. "And you'll die without ever knowing what was really going on."

I threw myself at him with a roar, which was stupid. If I'd kept my mouth shut he wouldn't have known I was coming.

Connie fumbled with her jacket pocket. The one-eyed man vanished, sending me charging into a brick wall.

"Blooded nails… What now?" said Connie dusting me off.

"This is all about people interfering with the Monument. You remember I said there was a machine made of streets? There's one place where we might be able to find the plans."

We went down a side street, behind yet another all-night supermarket. We reached a narrow gap between two shops: a cobbler, and something with windows full of stained glass. One of the buildings extended across the top of the opening, creating a narrow, low passageway.

We stopped outside a small wooden door. It was black from old tar that had softened in the warm breeze. A lumpy black iron knocker hung at head height.

"Here we are," I said. "Hang on."

I felt the magic instantly and it was barely an effort to trip the enchantment. The door opened with a hollow click. It was a square room. It was just my height, although Connie had to stoop to avoid the low beams. Cabinets crammed with herbs, powders and strangely shaped glassware lined the room. Odd creatures – puffer fish, crocodiles with human arms, clockwork monkeys – hung from the ceiling. The room stank of incense, with ribbons of grey smoke still hanging in the air.

"What's that?"

Connie looked down.

All the furniture had been pushed to the edges of the room, with a huge, intricate magical circle in the middle of the floor. There was a folding stool in the middle of the circle. I smiled. A green chalk summoning triangle took up the back corner, right up against the bare brick wall.

"Its a magical circle…" I said, "but it's different to the one we saw at the Monument. The stool is Danny's too."

I shrugged at Connie's baffled expression. "Summoning work takes ages, so Danny likes to have a sit down."

"When was he here?" asked Connie looking around. "Do you think we can still catch up with him?"

"The circle looks fairly fresh," I said, not wanting to

disturb anything. "It can't have been drawn much more than half an hour ago."

"Can you tell what he was summoning?" asked Connie. She peered at the symbols in the circle.

"I can see the symbol for Capricorn, and retrograde Saturn. Nasty. That's as much as I can work out," I said. "Summoning isn't my area."

"But it is His Majesty's?" she asked.

"You mean Danny?" I gave her a weird look. "Yeah, he's a chalk circle man, a conjurer. I've said that all along."

She looked at me like I was a moron, hands on her hips.

"No," she said. "I meant his Majesty King Charles II."

"Oh..." I said. "The King was into alchemy. But this room was for anyone who needed it. They put a bit of everything in here."

Ancient dried herbs and toxic alchemical powders sat in sealed containers. There was a small alcohol stove for heating the unpleasant compounds they liked working with.

"Start checking those drawers. We're looking for a set of paper plans. With any luck we'll be able to work out if we can restart whatever magic was keeping our fire spirit and its friend trapped under London. I'm going to take a look back at what Danny did here, see if I can work out what he was up to," I said.

Connie smirked a little. "If you start screaming, I'm going to leave you here."

"I'm sorry," I said rolling my eyes. "Are you ever going to let me forget that?"

"I will one day," Connie said. "Until then you can suffer."

"Fine."

I tried to clear my mind. "But you should feel guilty. I think I've saved your life at some point this evening."

Connie sniggered and climbed on a table to check the higher cabinets.

I took a deep breath and looked back. Over a hundred magical practitioners had used this room. Generations of conjurers and banishing circles had bleached the passage of time. Entire stretches of the past were gone or distorted beyond recognition. It was a queasy, disjointed vision. The clearest patches were where a conjurer was interrupted or had to leave in a hurry: I watched a bored and irritable demon amusing itself with an old Gameboy. I watched conjurers succeed and fail (a LOT failed and got eaten). Sometimes alchemists came and went, grinding powders and brewing potions. They were generally safer, but one of them managed to disintegrate himself.

Finally, I found Danny. He was buried deep in the jumbled up soup of time. I saw him sitting on his folding stool in the middle of the circle. His eyes were fixed on something I couldn't see, and his lips moved silently, breathing spells barely loud enough to hear. If I squinted I could just about see a blurry smudge in the air over the triangle.

"Esteban?" He looked up suddenly. "Are you watching me? Look, don't go to the Monument if you can avoid it, it's too dangerous. I've got a plan, but I need the right spot. Go to…" he faded out.

"Go to where?" I asked.

I pulled hard at the stream of time, grabbing it tightly. I got Danny again, the moment in time appearing like a half-forgotten memory, but I couldn't hold it.

"Dangerous…" he said.

I concentrated but it was no use; the moments slipped away as I tried to keep hold of them. "Don't trust…"

He was gone, and so was the rest of the time stream. A wave of power burned the past away. It was frightening and frustrating at the same time. I hung in an empty vortex as the room was wiped out.

There was nothing to do but bob back up to the present. I growled, which probably sounded less manly than I intended, and surfaced out of the cold, empty waters of time.

"My god, you're back," Connie said, adjusting her shades. "You actually physically vanished that time."

I took a step back, leaning against the wall. The air was hot and heavy like soup. There was a disgusting smell of rotten eggs.

"That was hard."

Spots flashed in front of my eyes again.

"Did you find what we were–"

Danny's voice echoed sourcelessly through the room, chanting words of power. I felt a cold flush.

"Oh no…" I had a bad feeling.

Connie shook me.

"I think you've set off a trap."

Chapter Seven

"Look at that!"

Connie pointed to the chalk triangle in the corner of the room.

"Did you find the map? Or a diagram? Anything?" I asked.

"We have a more important problem," snapped Connie.

Danny's triangle was active again. Dark, nauseating power flowed through it, going straight to the pit of my stomach. It had the distinctive feel of Danny's magic… but this was nasty. I felt something old and hateful notice us, pushing through the gap in the worlds towards the summoning space. From the way she had her hand on her mouth, I think Connie could feel it too.

"How is that happening?" Connie asked. "Is it a trap?"

"It might be." My mind whirled. "Or I might just have triggered it by messing with time."

"What?!"

Connie backed towards the door. "Blooded nails! Is that all you can do? You're like a blind sheep in a minefield."

Something was definitely forming in the triangle. It's a piece of magical trivia that not many people know about: circles are only for the summoner, triangles are for holding whatever it is that you've summoned. They always get it wrong in the films.

"I've probably triggered the ghost Danny's summoning," I said. "Like when you see ghosts that are just recordings of the past: phantom carriages and people who repeat their death in a loop. Most of it comes from clumsy time magic."

"Fantastic," Connie snapped. "Get rid of it."

We both felt the sensation of the spirit sliding through into our reality. It felt like having slugs in the back of your sinuses. The triangle pulsed and bulged. Something dark started to form inside.

"I wish it was that simple…" I said. "But I think it's taken an interest in us."

"Did Danny control it? Can we keep it in the triangle?" Connie asked.

It was in the triangle, but we were outside the circle. That made the chances of containing it pretty small.

"We'd better go," I said.

Connie turned and twisted the door handle.

"It won't open," she said. "What do I do now? What should I do? It's coming!"

It was starting to take on a vaguely humanoid shape. Its body was powerful but malformed. Its head had ears and horns. I had a bad feeling we'd seen it before.

"Hostia…" I tried to think of anything except my rising panic.

"Esteban!" Connie shouted, pulling at the doorhandle.

The thing in the triangle came almost all the way into focus. It had yellowish goat fur with longer red fur on its back and shoulders. There was a human-ish face on its chest, with sharp teeth and goat-eyes. Its body was out of proportion with its arms and legs – much too long – and it had the legs of a bull. Its head was a flopping tumour with the ears of a horse. There were claws and horns everywhere.

"It's a nightmare…" I said.

"Stop staring, you've seen it before," Connie hissed. "Do you want to help me get the door open?"

"You can get it open on your own," I said, without turning. "Just feel the lock and will it open."

"Help me! This nightmare's going to get loose!"

Connie gritted her teeth and put both hands flat on the door. "Please work…" she begged.

"I have to do something! "I hope this works," I said, reaching back in time.

The goat-wolf-nighmare pushed against the triangle. Without Danny to do the magic, it was like trapping a lion in a wet cardboard box. We didn't have much time. But I'm good with time.

The triangle would hold for literally one microsecond. I stretched it as far as I could and grabbed the nastiest fragments of the past I could find.

Two things happened at once, and for the first time that night they were both good.

First, Connie opened the door with a shout of "Success!"

Secondly, I threw three hundred years of magical disasters in the Portent's face.

Suddenly, the Portent was sharing the same space with every monster and explosion that had happened in the triangle for the past three hundred years. A bored, angry demon holding an old Gameboy materialised. A bat-like creature tried to appear; Aoel, the spirit who found treasure for the holy tried to appear as well; an alchemical explosion from 1862 detonated. Some spilled acid from a failed experiment made the spirits howl in agony. An ominous cloud of green gas seeped out of an old flask. Other magical disasters, less distinct than the first ones, started to play themselves out in the confined space. Sorcerers are good at making deadly mistakes. I threw fistfuls of them into the triangle just as it reached breaking point.

A clap of magical feedback powdered every piece of glassware in the room. All the carefully gathered alchemical ingredients turned into inert grey powder. The Portent howled.

We ran out into the street, making good time through Covent Garden Market.

"You were gone for hours," Connie said between breaths.

"Second line of defence," I said. "The City is holding time in one place."

"Is it intelligent?" Connie asked. "The City, I mean."

I shrugged.

"I don't know," I said. "It reacts to things. If it is intelligent, it's never spoken to us. Then again, if you had fleas, would you talk to them?"

We'd reached the cobbled open space around the market. Fine drizzle was making the cobblestones treacherously slippery, but I didn't feel like stopping yet. I slid, managing to avoid falling as I skidded off the pavement. A scream echoed through the market and the backstreets. Connie turned paler, if that was possible.

"I think our friend has got out of the mess I created," I said. "I was hoping it would go home once time snapped back to normal."

We turned onto the Strand. The sky glittered with burning pieces of wreckage whipped around on the Great Fire's weather system. They sparkled, vanishing as they reached the edge of the time distortion. The firelight made a false dawn from behind the buildings of Fleet Street.

Connie peered at the glow reaching high above the modern buildings and sighed.

"I can see the fire," Connie said. The hot wind blew in her face. "Is that bad?"

"It means the city can't hold it within the old boundaries of London," I said. "Considering that's where it's strongest, this is bad."

"How long have we got?" Connie asked.

"I don't know," I said. "Not long."

Somewhere behind us, the Portent howled.

We got to the Strand but time was changing here too. Faint ghosts of refugees rushed past us.

"The one-eyed man doesn't want us here. That might mean there's still something we can do."

"Right…" I said, cautiously.

"And I don't know if you've noticed," she said, "but we're basically between a rock and hard place."

Timewarped London had turned into a scene from hell. St. Pauls – now a blackened, broken gothic shell with a jagged, wrecked spire – was burning, and Ludgate Hill was glowing bright orange. All traces of Farringdon road – banks, restaurants and railway stations – had vanished leaving only burning 17th century buildings.

Streams of glowing white liquid – melted lead from the roof of St. Pauls – flowed freely down to the Fleet river. The water boiled where the molten metal touched it, sending up clouds of steam.

"Oh, that's rank." I covered my mouth with my sleeve. "That smell…"

The air was like a rotten Sunday Roast. That was why the Victorians had covered the Fleet: it was full of carcasses from the meat market. The fire had warmed the water.

What had been flickering shadows were now people, crowds heaving their goods up the hill. Even the buildings on our side of the Fleet were burning now, and most of them looked empty.

"That's the rock," I said. "Where's the hard place?"

Connie turned me around. The Portent stood a little way up the hill, capering towards us.

"This street was bombed in the war," I said, feeling back through time. "I can probably…"

"Please don't!" Connie snapped. "I haven't got that much faith in your aim."

"We've got to do something." I said. "Give me a better option."

The fire and the crowds of refugees reflected in her dark glasses. The fire was so bright that I could almost see through the lenses.

"Hang on…"

Connie looked at the Portent, then back at the crowd.

"The Dutch are coming!" she bellowed. I don't know why I was surprised, even her speaking voice was like a foghorn.

People stopped what they were doing and stared. Connie pointed up at the Portent, who either didn't understand what was going on or didn't care. He set a straight line and strode towards us. The crowds roared with fear and hate. I pressed myself against the wall, Connie stood next to me, as the refugees suddenly turned into a violent mob.

The Portent drooled, capered and giggled. When the crowd were a few feet away the creature made a sound like a blocked plughole. The closest figures collapsed, screaming as the monster vanished under them.

"What just happened?" I asked.

"You remember the war we were fighting?" Connie said. "It was against the Dutch."

"Right," I nodded. "So you're telling me that the crowd mistook the Portent for a Dutchman?"

Connie shrugged and held up a folded piece of paper.

"I think I found what we were looking for while you were away, " she said. "It's a map of London, with the sort of notes that Danny might understand."

At least for a few minutes, my day was looking up.

"That's awesome… We should head for the backstreets." I said. "It hasn't gone very well so far, but the fire might have made a mistake. If the people of 1666 are appearing, we might find some help."

Connie hesitated, but nodded hard and followed me. We walked down into Salisbury Place. Unlike in the city, there wasn't much difference between 1666 and the modern day: the houses here were made of brick and the streets were paved. The strangest thing was that someone had taken the trouble to hang lanterns outside some of the houses. They glowed like will-o'-the-wisps in the smoke.

"This is too much," Connie coughed. "There might not be anyone around."

"We'll have to be careful." I said. "It depends on where we are in the timeline. This is where people fought the fire."

My eyes were streaming from the constant cinders; I couldn't see Connie's eyes, but tears rolled down her cheeks.

"Are you going to be okay?" I said, trying to get a look around the edge of her shades. "Your eyes, I mean."

"Probably," she said wiping her cheeks and leaving white patches in the soot. "But I don't think either of us is going anywhere."

Explosions rumbled somewhere in the distance.

"They've started using gunpowder to fight the fire," Connie said. "That means we're on Monday or Tuesday. Do you think it'll stop when we get to Wednesday, the way the real fire did?"

I tried to think of what to say. The heat was almost unbearable. The modern day Salisbury Place was the headquarters of a multinational company. But in 1666 it opened up into a paved yard with a square building. Abandoned piles of goods – clothes, weapons, armour – were lying around. There were heaps of paper too, some already on fire. A massive papier mâché boulder sat burning fiercely.

"Every time I walk around a corner I get a new dose of 'what the hell?'" I said.

"It's just theatre stuff," Connie said. "They turned Whitefriars Monastery into the Salisbury Theatre. We should keep moving."

There was a sound on the other side of the yard. It was loud, but the other sounds made it hard to locate. Every building around us was burning fiercely, some of them were half-way to falling apart. The wreck of a white plastered mansion loomed over everything. Fire belched out of the windows of one of its towers.

"Connie!" I grabbed her.

The tower buckled, collapsing with a shower of burning debris. The sound of roaring flames, falling wood and shattered brick was so loud that it hurt.

"Watch out," I ducked, pulling my jacket over my head as I tried to shield Connie.

Something roared.

"That was weird, it sounded like an animal."

"That was an animal," Connie said. "A big animal."

I could have looked around in time and tried to work out what was going on, but it felt wrong. Reality was tight, like a piece of material stretched as far as it would go.

"So much fire." Connie was shaking. "I can't take much more of this," she whispered. "Can we just go?"

Whatever-it-was roared again.

I looked around wildly. "I'm warning you," I shouted. "If you come any closer I'll probably do something stupid."

"I'm getting away from here," Connie said. "And god help anything that gets in my way."

Connie growled like an animal and stood in front of me, crouched as if she was going to leap at something. She took a perfume bottle out of her pocket. A section of wall sagged and gave way, opening onto a cobbled alleyway. The crashing sound almost masked the roar of whatever beast was stalking us.

"Come on Connie," I whispered. "Don't go mad. Part of the wall there has collapsed. We can get straight into the Temple. We should be safe there."

Connie laughed and took the top off the bottle of perfume. It was a horrible emerald green colour.

"I'll destroy it," she breathed. "I can't take this anymore. I'll destroy it."

"Oh come on," I said. "Why does everything have to try and kill us tonight? It might be friendly."

A figure lumbered out from behind some papier-mâché boulders. It was half way between a huge man and a bear. The fact that it had a hat and coat on didn't make it any easier to decide which.

The one-eyed man stood next to it. Finally something had wiped the smile off his face.

"You're starting to vex me," he said baring his teeth. "Everything is going to plan, and yet I've still got you blundering around. If it was my choice, I'd just put a shiv in your bellies and feel you wriggling around… but himself wants things done a certain way."

Despite the heat of the flames, I suddenly felt cold.

"Who are you?" I asked.

The one-eyed man sneered.

"You've heard my name," he said. "While I was at my work on Middle Thames Street."

"Valentine Knight," I said. "The man Thomas Bloodworth was speaking to. You must be nearly four hundred years old."

"How?" Connie stuttered, trying to look away from the flames.

"You should be able to recognise a man who sold his soul," said the one-eyed man fingering his eyepatch. "With your experience."

I gave Connie a questioning look.

"What do you want?" I demanded.

"I remember him now," Connie said. "He tried to put in a plan to rebuild the city after the Great Fire but the king had him arrested."

A shadow passed over his expression. "The King's advisers disapproved of me. They felt I had some sinister, malevolent plan."

He stepped back, waving an arm with the air of a showman. "This is the Werebear of St. Brides. It was often sighted in the 1640s and 1650s, but never after the Great Fire of London." His expression darkened. "Let's hope that was because it died of food poisoning after eating you two. Kill them!"

The bear-man put his head down and charged.

Connie shoved me aside. I'd like to say I used the momentum to backflip off the wall and double scissor-kick it in the head, but all I did was hold my breath as it skidded past us. It roared and came around in a clumsy arc.

The werebear reared up on its back legs, blocking the street we'd come down. Connie shoved me back, staying in front of me.

"What are you doing?" I asked, glancing back towards the opening into The Temple.

The one-eyed man was gone.

"I'll kill it," said Connie.

She held out the perfume bottle. Her expression was manic.

"It isn't a bad smell. You can't get rid of it with perfume," I snapped.

"Who said this was perfume?" Connie said.

"What?"

The werebear shifted. Connie roared. Granted, she's taller than me, and her voice is incredibly loud, but it wasn't quite as impressive as when the werebear roared back.

It charged again. I flattened myself against the wall, getting a muscular shoulder in the stomach as it barrelled past, turning in a tight circle and squaring up to me again. It looked less human by the second.

Behind us, it sounded as if the Portent was finishing the mob. Cries of 'Dutchman!' had changed to screams. Dark fluid was flowing down the hill in constant waves, turning the soot into a river of gritty black mud.

I tried to reach for something I could use against the bear, but no bombs had fallen here in the blitz. This alleyway had been a perfectly safe street for hundreds of years.

The bear charged again. Connie sprayed green liquid into its face as it thundered into her. It bellowed and swiped at her. She flew through the air and hit the wall with a nasty, fleshy thump.

"Connie!" I cried, starting forward, but the bear was standing between us.

Her dark glasses fell off and I saw her eyelids, wet and black with heavy eyeshadow. There was something wrong with them, but I had better things to think about right now. Connie shrieked and dropped the perfume bottle, scrabbling for her glasses.

"No," she hissed, groping blindly with her eyes screwed shut. "Dammit!"

The bear thrashed around in agony. Its face burned with green light, outlining its horrible, half-human skull. It reared up, howling with rage.

"What have we ever done to you?" I shouted.

In the street outside, the shade of a Londoner staggered past. His skin was black with bulging pustules. His breath rattled in his chest. The Portent howled and laughed. I pushed down the hysterical urge to join in.

The bear growled, green vapour rising off its face. It glared at me through a mask of obvious pain before turning back to Connie.

"Aha!" Connie reached under a piece of smouldering timber, finding her glasses.

The bear roared. Connie put her glasses back on, but it was too late. In a second it would be on her.

The perfume bottle was too far away. It might as well have been in the next street.

All Connie could do was stare into the face of the angry black werebear.

"Blooded Nails!" she said.

I would have tried to do something. I would probably have tried to fold time around the bear and get her out of the way. It probably wouldn't have worked – the tension between the city's slow time and the Great Fire's speeded up time would have torn a hole in reality. I would probably have been stuck in a time loop, watching Connie die again, and again and again.

Instead, gunfire tore through the air.

It wasn't modern gunfire, this was the sound of black powder rifles. This was the kind of gun that had a range in feet instead of metres, and left very large holes in things. The bear flipped onto its back. For a moment it looked more like a burly man wearing a filthy black cape, then someone shot it again. The crack of a flintlock pistol rang through the air and the werebear vanished, bursting into greasy black smoke.

Connie crossed herself. It was a while before I could stop staring at where the bear had been.

A man stood holding a double barrelled pistol. There were other men with him. None of them bothered to try and reload their guns. Flintlock weapons are pretty much useless once you've fired them. They handed their guns to their servants and drew their swords.

All of them had the same look: long curly hair and filthy white shirts. They all had tight trousers with high boots. Most had as much extra weight as me.

They all walked behind their leader. He wasn't very tall or good looking, or muscular, but I've never seen anyone obviously so happy to be in danger.

"You girl." He looked Connie over. "Does your father know you're here?"

If it had been me, I'd have been asking what the gigantic bear-thing was. My heart was still trying to leap out of my chest. Connie curtsied and looked at her feet when she spoke to him.

"I doubt it," she said, quieter than normal.

"Well it is getting late… Fierce late. The city is burning from Cripplegate to the river. A pair of young cubs like you shouldn't be sent to do the work of men."

I saw Connie's shoulders tighten, but she didn't say anything. Surprisingly, the man noticed too.

"I shouldn't have said that," he said, handing his pistols to a servant. "It was unworthy of me. You may rise."

I tried to make eye contact with Connie, but her shades stopped me seeing if she was looking back at me.

"What afflicts your eyes?"

The gunman frowned.

"Are you blinded?"

"No, Your Grace," Connie said, still a lot quieter than usual. "I got these from an Italian, they protect my eyes from the soot."

"Oh. What will they think of next?" he said, turning to the other men and their squads of servants. "Alright lads, our sport is done. Back to it."

The others turned unwillingly and started making their way back across the yard. The man who'd saved our lives drew his sword, looking lovingly at the way it glinted in the firelight. He gave me a strange sidelong smirk.

"Methinks your being here is a very ill omen Spanish dwarf," he said.

"Umm… I…" I said.

Connie was looking at her feet.

"Umm… Connie?" I gritted my teeth.

She didn't say anything. The man with the sword paced around me.

"Spanish in aspect, but with London accents," he said. He turned the sword so that it flashed in the firelight. "You have clothes of fabrics which I have seen naught the like, and such fine blacks…" said the man with the sword, shaking his head. "Most strange of all, Lord forgive me for saying it, you know me not."

"Umm… ? I'm sorry about that," I said. "Should I?"

"'Tis nothing," he said, adjusting his cuffs. "Are you here to meddle, or is it you yourself that's enchanted?"

I didn't really have an answer to that. One of the things about time magic is that actual time travel is hard.

My personal best is about three minutes.

"You've seen people like me before?" I asked.

The man nodded.

"Aye, in a certain secret place with my brother. I have seen those like you appear and disappear before my eyes, oftentimes with great flashes of light."

"You've been in the workshop?" I asked.

"Aye," he smiled again. It was a slightly lopsided smile. "On Fisher's Alley. I like to indulge my brother's pastimes."

He wiped his free hand on his trousers. "Perhaps I should introduce myself: I am James Stuart, Duke of York. The workshop belongs to my brother the King."

I was half way through reaching out to shake his hand when Connie mimed a bow.

"Oh… that would make you a prince. Sorry again," I said bowing. "Your Grace. Sorry."

Connie mimed kissing his hand, but I decided not to. Thankfully, bowing seemed enough.

"And your name?" James asked.

"Esteban Fawkes," I said. "No relation to the man who tried to blow up your father. This isn't a plot, and I'm not a witch, in case you were thinking that."

He smiled the sort of knowing smile that only a face more handsome than his could get away with. Then he barked out a clipped, rough laugh.

"Rubbish," James said. "You ride the winds of time and bring me a creature that dares not show its face." He looked at Connie.

James gripped his sword and leaned in closer, grabbing a fistful of my shirt.

"The question is, are you our wizard or another's?"

His breath smelled of stale beer and tobacco. Now we were nose to nose I could see the scars on his cheeks, and the fact that he hadn't shaved. I also couldn't help focusing on the hand holding the sword to my face. It had a wide scar across the knuckle. The skin bulged with a strange, rubbery texture.

"Do you know the tale of that mark on my hand?" James nodded towards the scar. "I was aboard the Royal Charles, a day off Lowestoft. We were locked tight with the Dutch. The waves were throwing us about like a dollymop. Then the damned Dutch cannons threw chain at us."

I didn't know what to say except some plea for him not to cut me. His eyes clouded over with the memory, but he didn't relax his vice-like grip. I prayed that he didn't have some Restoration-era post traumatic stress disorder.

"Have you ever seen chain shot, boy? It swings like a scythe and cuts through men like butter. Good men like Boyle and young Berkeley..."

His face turned red. "The next thing I knew, I was wearing them like water in a tempest.

He filled my entire field of vision. I could feel the cords of muscle in his arm. He laughed another barking, violent laugh.

"I thought I'd been hit by a wave. Then I came to my senses with this cut. I've never since had the proper use of my hand. At first I thought it was the chain, but ..."

He stopped, coughing in the smoke. I was convinced that he was going to dice me up, but I wanted to hear the end of his story.

"...I saw the men look at me as if I was the devil.

This was no chain bite or the kiss of steel…"

He shoved his hand into my face. "This was a cut from when the chain broke open Boyle's head and spat his brains all out. This cut is from a piece of his flying skull."

I've faced off against murderous spirits, living fire elementals and beasts from out of time. None of that has the same kind of menace as a flesh and blood human sticking a piece of metal in your face.

"What do you think of that, boy?"

He smiled.

We stood in silence for what felt like hours. He watched me intently, his eyes glittering.

"Aye?" he said. "What think you? In truth?"

I said the only thing that came into my head. I don't know why I said it, but the moment I thought of it I knew the words had to come out of my mouth.

"Well…" I began, fighting back a terrified grin. "I can't help wondering how you got your clothes clean, because I've basically ruined what I'm wearing right now."

He didn't laugh, but some gear changed in his head. I'd half expected a booming laugh and a hearty slap on the back, but there was nothing. He just relaxed and dipped the point of his sword to one side.

"Good enough!" he said, letting me go and stepping away. "The cloth was silk. They burned it. Bloody waste of good cloth, really. Can't see why they don't use wool."

I was waiting for him to laugh, and for it all to be some sort of manly joke that soldiers play on each other, but apart from the tiniest smile he put his sword away and acted as if nothing had happened. I tried to share a glance with Connie, but she was still looking at her feet

"So," York asked. "Ours, or theirs?"

"Ours," I said. "Definitely ours."

"Very well," he said. "My brother has a whole murder of wizards. We'll join them, if ye can be of any use."

"A murder?" I asked, adding, "Your Grace."

He was already striding across the courtyard towards the gate into Whitefriars. I looked at Connie.

"What do you mean 'a murder?'" I asked again.

James' voice boomed out, "A murder: a collection of wizards! Come along, Master Fawkes."

He turned on his heel, hand on his sword. "And you, Changeling."

"Sorry," I said, trying to keep the annoyance out of my voice. "Look, if I'm going to help you I'd just like you to answer one question."

"Name it!" he barked.

"What was that thing that attacked us?" I asked.

James of York looked back at me as if I was either incredibly stupid or barking mad.

"'Twas the Bridewell Bear," he snapped. "You pudding-brained hedge pig, know you nothing?"

"Oi!" I said. "I'm from three hundred and fifty or so years in your future. And no, I've never heard of it."

York rolled his eyes. "And ye won't have, fool. Just this moment ago ye saw me kill the damn thing!"

Chapter Eight

After being terrified out of my mind for so long, I almost didn't notice when we finally made it out of Whitefrairs into the Temple itself.

Of course, the Temple isn't a temple. It has a church, but it's really just very expensive housing and offices for lawyers. Once it was the HQ of an order called the Knights Templar, but they suddenly got accused of being witches back in 1308 when a lot of people owed them money and couldn't pay it back.

It was quieter here, and for the first time in however long I didn't feel like I was in imminent danger. Part of it was knowing James could summon armed maniacs and kill supernatural beings.

We were coming up to a timber-framed building with two people outside. We reached the middle of a wide open courtyard, surrounded by brick buildings that were burning, but didn't look like they were going to collapse any time soon. The timber framed building divided the courtyard it into two halves. It wasn't on fire yet, but with so many burning buildings around it, and pieces of burning paper drifting on the breeze, it soon would be.

I realised that the people I'd seen were arguing, gathered around what looked like barrels. I had a horrible feeling.

I leaned closer to Connie, "Those barrels – that's

gunpowder, isn't it?"

Burning woodchips and paper drifted on the breeze, settling on the ground. One of them settled on a barrel.

"Great fire safety!" I said. "Wonderful."

I could see one of the two men standing by the barrels was a soldier, probably quite important. His coat was stained with soot, but it looked expensive. He had a sword buckled to his belt and he was wearing riding boots. He was holding what looked like a tool for lighting gunpowder.

A younger man with a weak chin and watery blue eyes stood in front of the soldier. He held a sheaf of papers like a weapon. He turned to greet James.

"Your Grace, God grant you mercy. "I am an apprentice at law," he said.

"Master Lawyer," James growled.

The lawyer raised his nonexistent chin.

"Is it the case that you intend to demolish Paper House with gunpowder?" he asked.

James looked at the soldier.

"Aye, I do Sir. Have you any quarrel with it Sir?"

The young lawyer's eyes glittered.

"As a matter of fact, I do," he replied unrolling the sheaf of papers. "I think you will find that in Paragraph Five of Chapter the Sixth of the Temple Charter that such action is illegal."

James, Duke of York, wasn't a theatrical man. He didn't growl or pinch the bridge of his nose. There was virtually no sign of what was about to happen but I could feel the oncoming violence.

He drew his sword with a ringing of metal on metal. The young lawyer honestly didn't seem to realise he was in danger. Looking at the future isn't easy, but I could see what was going to happen in the next few minutes.

It was Henry, the soldier, who saved the day. Before anyone could move, he swept his gunpowder-lighting-stick around in a neat arc that ended by hitting the back of the lawyer's head. There was a horrible crack.

The lawyer's eyes unfocussed. He collapsed like a puppet with its strings cut.

"You know," Connie whispered. "It's never safe to do that. Even people who are unconscious for a few seconds can suffer brain damage."

"Probably safer than not doing it," I whispered back. "Just this once, I mean."

I don't know if James heard us. I swear I saw one of his ears twitch, like a cat.

"You should be careful, Henry," James said. "He'll probably press charges for battery."

Henry laughed. "Shall I order the men to start putting the barrels into position?"

"No, it's better that you wait. I shall require instruction from master Hook." James sighed. "Cursed man must measure everything or he believes the world will end."

James shook his head and strode on, carrying us in his wake by the force of his personality.

He took us around the far side of Paper House. It was leafy here, and the buildings were untouched, despite the fact that it was raining cinders and burning paper. I could just about see the wavering edge of the time distortion on the other side of the courtyard. It was probably still the modern day in some of the houses. A small group of men were leaning around a folding table. One of them was powerfully built and hugely tall.

"Your Majesty," called James, quickening his pace.

The big man straightened up, his curly dark hair fell over his shoulders. His shirt was torn and filthy and his goatee was starting to grow out. He looked at us both with glittering blue eyes.

"Brother, approach me." He opened his arms, although James reached out and gripped his forearms instead of hugging him. "What news? Shall we destroy Paper House?"

James nodded.

"Your Majesty, if it pleases you. Also, mayhaps I introduce you to two foundlings of the fire? I bring you some familiar young girl, and Master Esteban Fawkes." He gestured from me to the big man. "Fawkes, this is His Majesty King Charles II."

"Mistress," Charles said. "Your eyes…?"

"I…" Connie bit her lip. "An Italian gave them to me. My father bought them, that is."

Charles' brows knitted a little, showing just a hint of tension to reveal that he wasn't buying her story. His expression of happiness turned to one of warm curiosity, as if he was the most innocent man in the world and couldn't possibly mean us any harm.

"They shine so, so black," Charles said. "Your father must have paid well for them, and in, what…? Lacquered wood, perhaps? I'll wager the lenses aren't glass."

Connie just nodded. Charles looked her up and down.

"For sooth…" He smiled warmly. "Your strange clothes and odd companion." He turned to me. "Taking no offence I hope, but you must understand that you seem as strange to me as I seem quaint to you."

"Umm…" I said. "I've never met a king before, so

please forgive me if I do something really rude."

He looked from Connie to me. There didn't seem to be any point in lying to him. If he was time-aware enough to see that I didn't look right then he was pretty sharp.

"By your leave," he said, as I tried to decide if I should look happy or sad. "But I must know something."

"Go on your Majesty," I replied, trying not to sound suspicious.

Charles' smile didn't slip, but I could see something moving fast behind his glittering eyes.

"As I asked." He pointed at the time distortion. "Could you read out what some ruffians have scrawled on those bricks?"

So that was his game. He knew I couldn't see the same wall that he was looking at. I wasn't even sure the buildings of the modern Temple had existed in the time when Charles was alive. I looked carefully into the past, scanning as quickly as I could, seeing back through the bands of compressed time until I saw the words that had been daubed there in 1666.

"'It was the French that done it,'" I read.

The King smiled. "I see, sir," he said. "So you have your letters? Fascinating. Do all the peasant boys read in your time?"

Chapter Nine

Inside, I kicked myself. He didn't need to prove that I could see the time distortion, cast spells or time travel. Just being able to read proved that someone like me was out of place.

"Yeah," I said. "That probably sticks out."

"As you say," Charles nodded, smiling. "So, Master Fawkes, since you have proved yourself a scholar and a sorcerer, you may come and meet two of my own."

There were two men standing by the folding table, each looking intently at the map laid out on it. There was a woman, too, covered from head to toe in grey silk, complete with a veil.

One of the men touched the veiled woman on the shoulder.

"If it pleases you to calculate the chances of the wind changing, Janey?" he said.

The second man noticed me noticing him and looked at me sharply, turning to his friend.

"Wren! Not in front of the newcomers," he grumbled.

Charles raised an eyebrow. The stocky man ignored him. The other man, Wren, blushed slightly and stepped away from the veiled woman, who didn't appear to either notice or care.

"Hook," James of York barked. "Where shall we place the charges to delay the fire?"

You'll wait your turn, we're scientists, not magicians," said the man, not bothering to look up from the map.

"I'll hear the answer when I ask for it," snapped James of York. "Or I'll have you clapped in irons."

"I'll tell you when I'm ready, or you'll be less use than Bloodworth," said Hook.

At this point Wren noticed Connie and waved a hand.

"Gentlemen," he interrupted. "Have a care for our company."

Hook stopped. "What? The girl? She must know how useless Bloodworth is. He couldn't put out his own wig if it was on fire."

James of York growled. "You two are no better," he said. "I have allowed you to come here and to bring…" he waved at the veiled woman. "Your hell-machine! Now you tell me that you can't even do the most simple of calculations?"

"And how would you know, m'lord York?" Hook rolled his eyes. "Did they teach you a lot of mathematics as a mercenary?"

"Better a mercenary than a coffee-drinking thief and braggart," James said. "Fighting talk doesn't mean ye can fence!"

King Charles was standing with a slight smile, watching the pair with visible affection. Wren watched for a moment, then brought the woman – the machine – over to join us. She made a faint ticking, whirring sound as she moved.

"Hello," Wren spoke to Connie first. "I must say, I'm honoured to meet you, I've long had a great deal of esteem for Master Bloodworth. He was an excellent Justice of the Peace."

"G-god grant you mercy," Connie's voice shook. "I think you might be the only one. This is my–" she stopped herself. "This is Esteban, I'm Connie–" she halted again. "I mean… I'm Constance."

"Your servant, miss," he took her hand and bowed. "I'm Wren. I've been charged with planning the demolition here for His Majesty."

"You are Sir Christopher Wren?" I said. "That's fantastic!"

Wren laughed. "Well, 'Sir' Christopher might be premature, but I hope my services will be of value."

King Charles II looked like he was keeping score of every time I polluted the time stream.

"Right," I said. "Well, you never know. I've got a lot of faith in you."

Wren bowed. The glow of the firelight made his pointed nose more prominent. He helped himself to snuff from a pewter box.

"So," I said. "Look… things aren't right."

Wren and the King exchanged a significant look. Charles dabbed at the corner of his mouth with a handkerchief.

"Janey?" Wren began, turning towards the machine. "Tell us of the time distortion."

The silk clothed woman nodded and began to speak.

"There is a most unwholesome distortion around the City of London, stretching almost to the far side of this yard, and for a goodly diameter around the city as a whole. Strength of the distortion polls at fifty-one gallohectres. I estimate that it is growing and will reach the City of Westminster by morning."

"I don't know if that's the same as the measurement we use," I said. "But the size sounds right. Look... someone set loose the Great Fire..."

Wren looked at his king. An uncertain look surfaced on Charles' face for a minute, quickly drowned under waves of polite smiling and quiet confidence. He stroked his beard.

"Young man, it isn't the Great Fire that you should worry about," said Charles turning away. "There has been something dark here for over a century. Since the time of Henricus Octavius: death, bloodshed and man turning upon man. Elizabeth's Doctor Dee tried to get rid of it; my grandfather, who knew of such things, did the same. The Great Fire was a... miscalculation."

Wren gave us a pained look.

"We thought we might flush whatever it was out of the city, but as you can see, we seem to have somewhat lost control. The Fire did chase the demon, rightly enough, but the dastard leads it a dance. We've lost half the city," said Wren.

"It has an ally," said Charles sighing. "For it anticipates our every move against it."

My heart leapt. "I know who that is," I said.

"Who?" Charles said.

"A man with one eye."

Charles seemed suddenly energised. "Brother! Hook! Your attention gentlemen," he called.

James of York and Robert Hook were still quarrelling when they were interrupted by a contrite looking King of the British Isles. Charles coughed, but they didn't react. I'm pretty sure that when a king coughs, everyone in the area who isn't a king is supposed to take notice.

"My calculations will be ready once you allow me to return to my job," said Hook to James of York. "Time that I spend in foolish prattle is time wasted!"

James of York raised an eyebrow. "Do my questions disturb you?" he sneered. "Well, I believe The Tower still stands. Perhaps the quiet there would suit you?"

Connie shook her head.

"I swear," she said. "They are the two rudest men in London."

"Look," I whispered to Connie. "I'm not stupid. Something's going on with you. Normal people don't keep acid in their perfume bottles. Who are you? Really?"

Connie's expression turned to annoyance. She adjusted her bright white hair and nodded at Charles. He was standing, dabbing the corner of his mouth as Hook and York argued.

...And he was listening to everything we said. He did a good impression of not hearing us, but I could almost see his ears pricking up.

Connie dropped her voice to a whisper.

"The King is a cleverer man than many give him credit for."

Charles tucked the handkerchief into his sleeve and clapped loudly.

"Pray, pardon me gentlemen," he said. "A moment?"

Hook and James of York dragged themselves away from their argument with the least grace I've ever seen, sweeping down into a pair of surly bows.

"Your Majesty," they said together.

"We have something to discuss with our new guests," Charles said. "Would you do us the pleasure of attending?"

James and Hook, not looking a bit sorry, nodded and took their places around the folding table. Charles gestured for Wren to take his place and offered his hand to 'Janey,' the machine-woman, guiding her to stand next to him. That left room for Connie and me. We looked down at an old map of London.

"The map is old," Wren said. "Over twenty years old." He glanced guiltily at the King. "The survey office have never stirred themselves to commission a new one."

"Really?" Charles raised an eyebrow. "Once this done, we shall see to it."

"Alas, there is a greater matter." Wren looked at us. "It might be best if our young friends, who have walked through the fire in their own time, tell us their tale."

So we did. We told them all about the Great Fire, the Portent, the time distortion, and the one-eyed man.

"Fie," James of York said. "How can we give them help? We have a city of our own to save."

Charles shook his head. "There is a London in almost three hundred and fifty years, brother. We owe it a debt. This is our fault."

"Why has it come back to burn in our time…" said James of York. "I don't understand!"

Charles tilted his head. "Think brother," he said. "Perhaps in the future the buildings are made of stone instead of wood. Perhaps our laws after this event change the way our subjects build. How starved of fuel would such a beast as the Great Fire be in that time?"

James of York didn't take long to get the implication. "It comes to eat, and when the beast returns–"

"Aye!" Hook completed the thought. "When it returns

The City of London will be engulfed with a mile-and-a-half wide blanket of fire. At an estimate."

We stood in silence as the idea sank in. With a fire storm on that scale it wouldn't matter that modern London was less flammable. The city would be engulfed in the sort of fire it hadn't seen since the second world war.

Connie chewed her fingernail and looked at me.

"Maybe your grandmother should just seal the city off," she muttered.

I didn't have much to say to that. Charles paid close attention to his own people, not appearing to watch us.

"Wren?"said Charles, tucking his handkerchief into his sleeve. "What of this strange twist in time?"

"Yes..." Wren said. "Of course, well... If Janey speaks right, the forces will split apart, but I believe it won't wait so long."

"We don't have long," I said.

James filled a clay pipe and lit it from a piece of burning paper that had fluttered down near to the table. There was a curl of bitter tobacco smoke. He puffed and stared thoughtfully into the distance.

"Which brings us to the question of the one-eyed man," James said. "If he's ambitious enough for necromancy his power will be formidable."

"And," Charles said, "the matter of the vile spirit who always seems a step ahead of us."

James smiled grimly. "This one-eyed man would seem to be the human agent," he said. "Perhaps we should speak with him."

"Send out messengers to find the one-eyed man," James said. "Let us see how much black magic he does when he's been hanged, drawn and quartered."

"No." Charles shook his head. "We'd lose what progress we made with the fire. Our place is to tame the blaze. We brought it here to fight this Portent, it is our duty to control it."

"Just don't summon another beast to fight it," I said. "Or this could turn into the old woman who swallowed a fly."

"So, what is the Portent?" Connie asked.

Charles looked thoughtful. "I believe it is a demon. It feeds on war, death, pain and misery. It makes brother turn on brother and makes men to hate each other. When they do, it grows stronger."

At that moment, the soldier Henry Jermyn ran over. His face was red from shock and anger.

"What's wrong? Speak honest Henry," demanded the King.

Henry nodded soberly. "Our men have been attacked. It was monstrous, Your Grace..."

"Don't tell me," I said. "Red and yellow fur, face in its chest, generally horrible to look at?"

"Yes!" Henry nodded.

"Your men," Connie asked. "Were they...?"

"Two frozen to death, another rotted by disease before my very eyes," said Henry as he crossed himself.

"Is there anything we can do to stop the Portent?" Connie asked.

"We have tried. We have years upon years of noble trying. What do you think, gentlemen?" Charles looked at Wren and Hook, who both nodded.

"Perhaps," Wren said. "We could build a circuit, using the geometry of the streets."

"Make a summoning circle, from the streets of London?" I asked.

"It could work," said Wren. "But it would have to be of great size to contain the Portent. The sides of the triangle alone would need to be a mile long."

Charles stroked his beard. "It must be done fast. How quickly could you draft some designs?"

"Well…" Hook rubbed his hands together. "With his majesty's permission, almost immediately. Perhaps on a grid system…"

"No." Wren shook his head. "The pattern on the streets must form a circle. When we rebuild London, its streets will form the machine that will trap this devil."

"Umm, I have a feeling I know how this is going to pan out," I said. "Could I ask you a question? Just off the tops of your heads?"

Connie gave me a knowing look and got the map out. We held it between us, trying not to let Wren or Hook get a look at it. I didn't think of shielding it from Charles, not at the time.

"We need to know something about your machine," said Connie. "Is there somewhere it'll be controlled from?"

"Please," I said. "Give us a way to reset things and put the Portent back in."

Wren puffed on his pipe and looked at Hook, who nodded. "St Paul's Cathedral, I should think. Wren?"

"Yes, yes," he said. "A grand machine." He bowed to the King. "With your majesty's permission."

"It's clever," said Charles stroking his beard. "but it leaves you without the answer to your own problem. If our machine is built in your time, from the streets of the city… then the monster is already free."

"It's hanging around London, for some reason," I said. "And so is the one-eyed man. There's still something it wants."

Connie adjusted her shades. "We still haven't found Danny," she said. "He might have a plan."

I looked at the knot of men who would shape the face of London.

"If you were a conjurer and you had a plan to either summon the Great Fire, or to bind the Portent, where would you go?" I asked.

To my surprise, it was James of York who answered. "He'd need space and flat, soft ground," he said. "If it were me, I'd make my way to Smithfield, outside Newgate."

I glanced at Connie, still wondering if I could trust her. "Let's see if Danny really does have a plan."

Chapter Ten

Stepping back out onto Fleet Street, there was no sign of the Portent. The people had gone too, the only sounds being the roar of the fire and crash of falling buildings. The river still hissed from the molten lead. It was littered with burning debris. I tried not to breath too much of the stinking, greasy steam. The heat was nearly unbearable. Across the river, the flagstones of Ludgate Hill still glowed orange. Connie looked at it thoughtfully.

The air raid sirens had stopped.

Connie gave me a tired look.

"They've stopped, but knowing our luck that's probably bad, isn't it?"

Even with a chance of things looking up I was too tired and afraid to be tired or afraid anymore. I grunted. Connie got the message.

"I thought so," she said.

She stared at the bubbling river for a minute. "You could stabilise this, couldn't you?" she said. "If you concentrated, we could make a bubble of time around us, which would mean we could walk across Farringdon Road and through the city like normal. It would be the fastest way."

"I'm too tired," I said.

Connie put her fists on her hips.

"We wouldn't have to hold it all the way, just long enough to get off Ludgate Hill and towards the walls."

I shook my head.

"Look," I said. "By now Newgate will be on fire. Greyfriars Monastery has actually exploded from the heat and there's molten lead flowing down the hill. We don't know if we'll be able to get through at Newgate. Remember: at this point it's still a wall with a gate in it."

"Oh come on," Connie shouted. "Don't be so wet. We should take the most direct route."

"Look, while there's no-one trying to kill us you and I need to talk," I said.

At that moment a guttural laugh drifted over the sound of the burning buildings. The Portent was back. My stomach sank.

The mob had done more damage than I'd expected: the Portent was covered in cuts and bruises, with a nasty wound over one of the eyes in its chest. Its slack, sharp toothed mouth was stuck in a loose grin, but there was no amusement in its eyes. It wasn't playing anymore. Now it was angry.

It hissed. Its goat-eyes flicked from place to place, always coming back to us. Connie clutched her dark glasses to her face.

"We should run," she said. "How fast can you do your time magic thing?"

"I can't–" I started.

I heard the Devil's ringtone, but it was too late to do anything. The Portent reached out a hand and a jet of filthy water cut through the air between us. Everything it touched started to rot. Connie grabbed my hand and pulled me towards the river Fleet.

"I hate that thing," I said, and I tried to gather my strength.

The Portent urged us forward with one pressure-hose blast after another, scouring the filth and soot off the street. Even the cobblestones bubbled and rotted away. Stones hatched into clouds of flies and knots of transparent worms. Connie tugged me towards the river, a blast arching past us and hitting a wall, collapsing it into a shower of maggots.

"Connie!" I said. "That thing seems to control dirt. That's what these worms are: people thought they spontaneously grew out of dirt."

"Esteban," said Connie, hustling me along. "You can tell me later."

The fire was trying to reach for it, but the monster knew where to stand. It kept to a narrow path in the middle of the street, tongues of flame bending towards it but never quite getting close enough to touch.

"You don't understand," I said. "Think how much muck and disease is in that water. We really don't want to be near there."

The Portent opened its mouth wide. There was a sound like rushing floodwater and I could feel a magical tightness in the air. The Devil's ringtone chimed over everything. The water's edge crept towards us.

"Esteban?" Connie stopped, bumping against me. "Stop giving it ideas."

The river Fleet became a mass of wriggling water-tentacles. Slabs of rotten grey fat detached themselves from where they'd solidified. Animal skulls – pig, cow and goat – rose out of the depths and rolled on the thrashing mass, glaring at us emptily. Tendrils of filthy water reached out towards us.

One of them wrapped itself around Connie's ankle. She screamed. There was no way the others would hear us from here, even if they hadn't been swept away on the winds of time. What refugees weren't horribly injured screamed and scattered into the backstreets. The Portent's face split into a grin.

Connie screamed again, one hand clamping her glasses to her face and the other reaching out to me. I pulled her close. The tentacle tugged hard, nearly pulling me off my feet, but I'm heavy.

"Do it," she said. "Do it now, change time now!"

"It's not that easy!" I said.

The tentacle yanked again and we fell, hitting the paving stones hard. Rubble, nails and shards of timber dug into me. I tried to drag Connie back up with me, but it yanked again. We slid towards the water.

"Nonononono!!!" I tried to kick my brain into giving me an idea. Any idea.

A watery limb hit me hard. It felt like falling onto the sea from an aeroplane. The fire roared around us. I could almost see a huge face forming in the heat haze above St. Paul's. It raged as the Portent hopped from one foot to the other, barely out of its reach.

"Hostia!' I said. It's a Spanish word. I got it from my grandmother. When the chips are down I swear like an elderly Spanish lady.

"Stop!"

I grabbed a heavy piece of wood. Connie was still holding on to me.

"No!"

We slipped further towards the river. Two more tentacles wrapped around my legs.

Connie dug one hand between the cobbles, fishing in her pockets with the other hand until she found a perfume bottle full of red liquid. She took it out and sprayed the contents onto her clothes.

The tentacle lifted us, smacking Connie against the floor until she dropped the bottle.

"Connie!" I yelled.

I didn't need to see Connie's eyes to see her fear. I wasn't much better. My legs were scalding from the hot water, and the rest of me felt like it was cooking from the fire. This close to the Fleet the smell of melting fat made me want to be sick.

A few feet away, the Portent grinned viciously. Its tentacles tugged again. We slid down the street, dragged over rubble towards the water's edge. It gave a tug and yanked Connie into the water, up to her hips. She shrieked, higher and louder than before. Water bubbled around her. Connie howled with fear and pain. I scrabbled at the flagstones, desperately trying to get a grip and keep us from getting any further into the water.

"Please!" Connie said. "You have to try!"

I took a deep breath and looked up at the Portent.

It gurgled out a laugh and stepped closer. Tongues of fire strained to touch it, defying all laws of physics as they snaked horizontally through the air, reaching from every burning object in the street. The Great Fire's face was fully formed over St. Paul's, a mask of useless rage.

The Portent laughed again.

Time magic comes naturally, but it's tricky. With water-tentacles trying to drag me into a boiling soup of dead animal parts I was never going to pull off something fiddly. On the other hand, pulling things out of the past or sending them away is fairly easy. So I grabbed a big chunk of burning building and sent it back as far as I could. The front wall of a shop vanished back into the 1400s. The Portent gurgled as the building dropped on of it like a falling tree.

I jumped back, putting my arms over my head. Brick and mortar smacked down with an almighty crash, showering the street with burning wood and masonry. A chunk of flying plaster bruised my arm and hit Connie a glancing blow on the cheek. A massive lump of stone wallowed through the air and dropped into the Fleet with a 'glop.' The Portent vanished under the wreckage.

Tongues of fire fell with a whoosh of combustion. Waves of heat sent me staggering back as the Great Fire hit the wreckage with the force of a blast furnace.

I might have been wrong, but for a second it sounded like the Great Fire was laughing.

The water tentacles had vanished the second I'd dropped the building on the Portent, so I rushed over to Connie.

"Connie?" I said. "Connie? Lie still for a minute, I want to see if you're burned."

"I'm not hurt," she said, face down on the flagstones.

I felt a sinking feeling in my stomach. "It doesn't hurt?" I asked.

"No," Connie said. "I'm not hurt. I'm fine."

I grabbed her foot and dodged out of the way when she tried to kick me in the face. I forced the leg of her jeans up; I was expecting a mass of partially boiled flesh and loose, dead skin.

She really was fine.

"You really are okay," I said as I dropped her foot. "You're soaked, but you're okay."

"I told you," she said. "I'm fine. Just give me a minute to rest."

"Those perfumes, that's alchemy, isn't it?" I said. "Who are you?"

Connie didn't say anything, she propped herself up on one elbow, breathing hard.

She gave me a hard look. "We've got a job to do, and it means we've got to stop all this. It doesn't matter who I am. If I was working with either the Portent or the one-eyed man they wouldn't be trying this hard to kill me."

She glanced at the fire, shaking herself free. "Look, I promise on all that's holy, I'm not trying to trick you. This isn't my scheme, and if it was I wouldn't have needed Danny. I've been around long enough to know other conjurers."

"I never accused you of any of that," I said. "I just want to know who you are and how long you've lived."

She looked at the fire again.

"Long enough that I saw this first time around."

It felt like the ground was slipping out from under me.

"Who are you?" I repeated.

Connie shook her head. We stared at each other for a few minutes. I don't know how long it really was, but it felt like forever. Connie didn't look like she was going to say anything else whether I gave up or waited until doomsday.

"This isn't over," I said. "But you're right: we've got better things to do. Are you okay to stand?"

She got up slowly, fighting hard to control her breathing as the fire raged all around us. We had a lot more clear space than before but the sight of the fallen, burning building seemed to freak Connie out a bit.

"It's not really under there, is it?" she asked, peering under the rubble.

"Probably not," I said. "Things like that don't have to stay in any one location. They only have a body if it makes their life easier."

"It controls disease," said Connie. "We had a plague the year before the Great Fire. Do you think His Majesty and the others summoned the Great Fire to chase out the Portent?"

"They said they did," I replied. "But they also said it had been here longer: someone called Doctor Dee tried to get rid of it, and so did Charles' grandfather, James I," I said.

Connie nodded.

"James I wrote a book about magic and witchcraft, but I didn't think he believed in it by the time he was King of England."

I watched the tongues of flame withdraw from the charred wreckage.

"Maybe he just found out the real story." I said.

"Esteban." Connie put a hand on my shoulder. "I will tell you everything, this just isn't a good time."

"Whatever. We should get going." I said.

"Shall we try the time stabilization?" Connie asked.

"I'm starting to feel like every time I disagree with you something tries to kill us," I grumbled as I took her hand. "But if you've been alive three hundred and fifty years I'm going to pretend you know what you're talking about."

All magic is vibration. I closed my eyes and tried to feel the frequency of the time spell the Great Fire was using. It was easier than I'd expected.

"Alright," I said, trying not to lose the thread. "This is the super-complicated version of a really easy spell: I can send things into the past or pull them into the future really easily. This time I'm going to be grabbing a moment, holding it for a second, and then grabbing another one. If I do it really well, it'll be like a cartoon – lots of stills making a single moving image."

"What if you don't?" Connie asked.

"Don't think about it," I said. "Hold my hand."

Connie took a deep breath and gripped my hand. For once she didn't crush my fingers.

"And... now." I said. "Here goes nothing..."

I tried to make myself as still as I could, so still that the spell flowed through every piece of me. Every cell in my body buzzed along with the magic.

"Here we go..." I said as I stretched the spell.

Connie glanced sideways. "It's working," she whispered.

I could feel normal road under our feet. I could still see the glowing flagstones on Ludgate Hill, but the smell and the heat couldn't penetrate our bubble of normal time.

"Okay," I took a step forward. "No matter what happens: no loud noises, no drama, and no distracting me, or we'll be plunged back into 1666 and either boil or burn to death."

Connie nodded, holding her breath. We stepped forward.

Despite all my warnings to Connie, it was nearly me who messed everything up. My second step brought us up to modern street level, rising up through the air. I yelped with surprise and the bubble of normality flickered threateningly. Connie didn't move, careful not even to gasp. I closed my eyes, barely holding it together. We bobbed in place for minutes, Connie standing very still and me trying to control my breathing.

"Right," I said. "Yeah, the Victorians put the Fleet under thirty feet of concrete. I remember now."

The corner's of Connie's mouth twitched up. I could feel the fine tremble of laughter rippling through her body.

"Don't worry," she said, struggling to keep a straight face. "I'll make sure I keep quiet and don't distract you."

We walked on a rough circle of tarmac high above the river. I could have fixed it so that we could see the modern world instead of the time distortion, but I didn't want to push myself.

"And this is the moment when I hope there aren't any cars around," I said. "Because otherwise we could end up as one of those ghost stories where someone hits a pedestrian, but when they stop there's no trace."

I took another step. This wasn't going to work if I had to shuffle the whole way. Connie did her best to match my pace. A breeze passed through the cool air of our modern bubble. With any luck, the city defences would still keep people off the streets.

We managed a slow walking pace. The river slowly turned into riverbank and the start of Ludgate Hill.

Birds rained down. They were real enough here that we could see them falling, twisting through the air as their wings burned. Their horrible squawks were barely covered by the roar of the fire.

"Okay," Connie said. "Just up this way and around the corner, there's a street that leads right to The Old Bailey."

And we walked. The air around us was the cool, night air of 3am, but in 1666 it was blisteringly hot: the white-hot rivers of lead still flowed down the street. From here we could see St. Pauls burning, its stones glowing as bright orange as the flagstones on the street. Our little bubble was dark, but in 1666 the night was almost as bright as day. If I lost it here we'd be fried alive. I gave myself a dirty look for thinking it. Connie looked sideways at me, but she didn't ask what I was thinking.

The Great Fire was frantic. It had obviously realised that the Portent had escaped. Unfortunately the Portent's smell was on Connie and me. That's the problem with huge, ancient fire elementals: they're not much brighter than dogs. Tongues of flame stretched towards us, unable to exist in my bubble of time.

I walked along with one hand out. I had a vague memory that there would be a wall coming up that didn't correspond with the street layout of 1666, and I was right. My hand came up against smooth white stone and we felt our way along it, backtracking until we found the street we needed.

Time pressed in on us from all sides. Sometimes I think time is alive. If it was, it didn't like what I was doing. I forced a breath and kept walking, feeling like a submarine at the bottom of the sea.

Outside my bubble the Great Fire roared at us from every burning building. Faces appeared in the flames and howled.

"Do you think we can reason with it?" Connie whispered.

"I know. It does seem a bit irrational." I said. "That's the problem with randomly unleashing things. You think you can control them. They obviously trained it well enough to hate anything that has magical energies like the Portent."

We were almost where we needed to be. The fire leapt, passing through a space where, in 1666, we didn't exist. It tried to find where I was in time. I dodged, sliding back a year and forward again into the present. Fire passed through us, visible but harmless. A near miss. It roared and crackled. A building shattered, throwing burning timbers onto a spot where we wouldn't be standing for over three hundred years.

Connie didn't make a sound but her fingers were as stiff as twigs. She looked around, trembling with the effort of containing her fear.

"The gates of Cripplegate were open by now," she said. "Are they closer than Newgate?"

"In the modern world?" I muttered. "I can't remember."

The strain of doing so much mental calculation was starting to get to me. I put one foot in front of another and stumbled, nearly losing the bubble. Painful heat battered us. I accidentally stuck my arm into 1666. Pain filled my world. Choking smoke burned my lungs.

"Hostia! Madre de Dios…" I whimpered, trying not to think about it. "I'm okay. I'm okay."

My sleeve was smouldering. The pain from my hand was unbelievable.

"Oh, come on…" I said, trying not to look at my hand. "Sorry. Nearly there."

"Shall we go to Cripplegate or Newgate?" Connie asked again. "Cripplegate is probably quicker."

"Danny is at Newgate," I said.

The pain from my hand was incredible.

"But," Connie said. "Cripplegate is quicker. Bloodworth is at Cripplegate."

I could hear the edge of panic coming into Connie's voice as the fire swooped and dived at us, passing harmlessly through where we would one day be standing. The goat-wolf-thing's face formed in the burning heart of a building.

"That's not us," I said. "Yeah, we've accidentally summoned it and been in the room with it with a few times, but that's definitely not us."

My hand. Oh god, oh god, oh god it hurt.

Connie nodded and closed her eyes.

"We can do this."

"If we could just speak to it," I said. "We could sort all this out."

I put one foot in front of the other. 'Walking' wasn't even the right word for it by now: I was just trying to put one foot in front of the other without falling on my face, like a scout for the zombie apocalypse. I think I was squeezing Connie's hand too tightly, because she swore. At least it distracted her from being afraid of the fire.

Around us, the Great Fire raged and burned. We'd come out into a wider street, leading down to where the remains of Newgate Prison burned fiercely. Drifts of rubble littered the streets, blazing.

"I can't hold it," I said. "It's too far."

Not to mention the pain in my hand. (Please don't mention the pain in my hand.)

It was getting harder to rise above the pain. I hadn't looked at my hand, but I knew it was bad. Pain, and fear of pain were expanding like a virus, taking up more and more of my brain. The fire followed us, shaping the flames into a crude face.

"Come on," Connie said. "Just a bit further."

I tried, but I could already smell the bitter smoke and taste the ashes on my tongue.

My hand. Was I going to lose my hand?

"I can't," I said.

I gritted my teeth. "It's too much."

The road under our feet changed from cold tarmac to hot earth. Gusts of hot air blasted our faces, almost cooking our skin. The pain was unbelievable. I just wanted to curl up around my hand and whimper. Was that what it would feel like, when the fire got us? We'd be destroyed instantly, but if you're burning 'instantly' is a long time.

"You have to," Connie's voice broke into hysteria. "If you drop the effect we'll both die."

"I can't," I said. "Run!"

The heat and smoke of 1666 burst into our carefully constructed sphere of time. What had been a muted sound of roaring, crackling fire suddenly hammered us with leaping flames and cracking timbers.

The fire roared. It moved fast, but it still had to go from fuel to fuel. We did what the Portent did: we ran as hard as we could, ducking away from the piles of burning wood and trying to stay in places where it couldn't go.

Unfortunately, we were still in the middle of the Great Fire of London.

"Esteban!" Connie yelled.

The fire curved around and tried to drop a building on me. I scrambled out of the way, sending a chunk of burning timber into the past before it hit me. The buildings either side of the fallen tenement house collapsed into the gap, crashing together drunkenly and falling into the street. The sound of shattering walls and tearing wood was deafening.

It was so loud that I almost didn't hear the sound of Newgate Prison falling on me.

Its huge stone wall had started collapsing. I babbled something. It wasn't fair. I'd survived all this, and now I was going to be crushed like a bug. That's the problem with the Devil's ringtone, it only seems to happen around magic. If someone sneaks up behind me with a brick in a sock, it stays quiet.

I closed my eyes.

Something moved me. I screamed in agony as someone grabbed my burnt hand, gripping it tightly. For a while there was no fire and no wall, just the pain in my hand.

The world shook.

Someone let go of my hand. It didn't do anything to the pain. This was the kind of pain that liked to hang around, just in case you needed something. After a minute I could see straight enough to realise I was alive.

Connie was standing close, with the shattered wall all

around us. She'd managed to shove me under a window. Thankfully it had been open, or we would have died horribly.

"Liquid alacrity," said Connie, holding up a bottle. "I'm running out of supplies."

My heart pounded so hard it felt like it might rip out of my chest. The fire raged all around us… but it couldn't come near. It licked at the stones, unable to get any closer.

We were within sight of the 'New Gate'. It was clear, and the gates were already open. The smile spread across my face. As painful as my hand was, things were looking up.

The Great Fire roared. Every part of it leapt and hissed with rage. Piles of rubble burned with a blue-white flame but the volunteers, soldiers and noblemen who worked here had cleared a space with gunpowder. They'd swept the debris so far away that even the wind couldn't spread the flames.

I moved fast. Partly because I wasn't sure that the Great Fire couldn't really get me and partly because there was a hospital on the other side of the time distortion. Saving the city was starting to feel a bit less important than saving my hand.

We ran, curving around a rough corner made from tightly organised piles of burning wreckage. The Great Fire lashed out, but there was still a clear path where we could be safe from the flames. I could see that Connie was keeping down so that she wouldn't leave me behind.

"You can go," I said, almost managing to talk and run at the same time. "We should be safe."

"If that's true," Connie said. "It's okay to stick

together, agreed?"

I was trying to think of a reply when we rounded the corner into the mouth of Newgate. In 1666 it was a solid stone barbican with some kind of offices above it. Thankfully the gates themselves had been removed, leaving it wide open. Soldiers with pikes stood outside. For a minute I thought they were going to try and stop us, but once they saw Connie they stood out of the way.

My heart leapt: I could see the modern world on the other side of the gate.

And Danny.

He was standing in the middle of a blue flaring light. His hat was long gone and his jacket flapped in the wind.

As we got closer it was obvious that the flare was light from a circle and triangle, spray painted directly onto the pavement. It wasn't really legal but the people would probably forgive him, considering he was trying to save the city. His voice boomed:

"...Angel of voices," he said. "Light and truth. Angel of Mercury and Thoth, God of scribes, left eye of the moon, Lord of Time. Angel of Mercury, by Raphael's grace you have been given leave to come. By the purity of this place and sweet scents in my circle, by the borrowed powers under my feet. Angel of Understanding, appear!"

This is the thing with chalk circles: they don't have to be chalk, and they take a long time to get right. Once you do, the results are impressive.

If the fire hadn't turned day into night the circle would have. The blue light mingled with the firelight to give me two shadows.

Space opened and closed. It wasn't the same as when we'd accidentally summoned the Portent. This was just a flutter, like someone stepping through a curtain.

The Angel appeared. It didn't look human. It had two arms and two legs, but that was about it. Its head and neck were bird-like with white feathers and a long, curving beak. The rest of it was painfully thin and covered in blue and white feathers.

Beady black eyes examined us intently.

"Danny…" I whispered. "What have you been up to?"

The Angel settled into the circle and the light died down. I could feel the magical energy going back to normal, only the wrongness of the time distortion wavering next to us.

My hand was hurting more than anything I'd ever felt before. It probably wasn't a good sign. It was about then I noticed how dizzy I was, and how cold I was.

To make things worse, the ground was being strange under my feet: it kept trying to sneak up on me like a game of Granny's Footsteps, running back whenever I gave it a dirty look. I decided to lean on the wall so that I could keep a better eye on things. Unfortunately my legs were being lazy and I ended up sitting on the pavement.

"Esteban," Connie said, stepping towards me.

Danny finally noticed us, turning in the circle.

"Esteban," he said, smiling. "Hang on a second, mate."

I thought he was going to order the Angel to help us, or send it away and come out himself. Connie gave him a smile, slipping her arm around my shoulder and trying to help me up.

"Connie," he said. "I didn't see what happened to you when the column went up. I'm glad you're okay."

"No thanks to you," Connie said, without any anger.

"I've been thinking about that," Danny said in his understated way.

Connie helped me half way to my feet. Once I was almost upright the rest of my body remembered what it was for. I waved Connie away and stood – really shakily – on my own.

I gave Danny a strange look. He had his 'I'm going to do something really impressive' expression on his face.

Connie took another step away from me, looking from Danny to where I was just about managing to stand.

"Dan," Connie said. "Are you alright?"

Danny gave us that little smile again. I heard the Devil's ringtone yet again. A cold flush came over me.

"Dan?" I stepped towards him.

"I'm fine," he said. "Madimiel! Bind her up!"

"What–" Connie started.

The Angel turned its head and blue light flared out behind its eyes. The pavement sizzled as lances of white light etched a triangle pattern into the tarmac. Connie's voice was drowned out by the sound of magic tearing the fabric of reality.

Connie turned towards Danny, a look of irritation and panic on her face. She was trapped in the centre of a binding triangle.

Danny smiled a tiny smile. "Now," he said. "Who are you really, where do you come from, and why did you release the Great Fire?"

Chapter Eleven

Connie gave Danny a withering look, but I could see how pale she was. Her lips had drawn back to reveal her perfectly white teeth, and her hands were balled into fists.

"Daniel," she said. "Look at Fawkes. We've got more important things to worry about."

"He'll be alright," Danny said. "Anyway, I don't think there's anything more important now than finding out who you really are."

I would have disagreed if I'd had the energy. Connie tapped her chin.

"I wonder, how long can you maintain two triangles? Will it be longer than it takes for that fire to burn London? Or can you keep it up until Esteban's grandmother seals the city?"

Danny smiled back. It was a genuine sort of smile, like the two of them were sharing a private joke. For some reason it made me really angry.

"Look, will you just tell him?" I snapped at Connie. "Because I really need to go into that hospital and I can't walk on my own."

"We've been going out for eight weeks, you'd think he'd have noticed," Connie said. "You've only known me for a few hours and you've got it almost all worked out."

Danny smiled again, putting his hand in his pocket. "I can make you tell me," he said. "I've got the angel this time."

"It's not like that," Connie said. "I'm not anyone dangerous, I just like my privacy. Anyway, I don't know you well enough yet. You might freak out."

Danny gestured at the angel.

"I think I can take a bit of weirdness."

Connie frowned sourly.

"You'd be surprised. Anyway, what were you doing back at the old alchemical laboratory? Why did you try to summon the Portent?"

"Hang on, yeah…" I glared at Danny. "Was that a replay of your handiwork?" I asked.

Danny gave me his patronising 'you don't see the big picture' look, which usually came before his 'sorry you can't understand my heartbreaking genius' apology.

"Don't even start," I said. "You were too busy trying to leave messages in time. How much time did you waste putting those together when you could have just phoned me and told me what was going on."

"Look," Danny said. "I forgot to charge my phone, alright? I thought I was coming out on a date, not getting involved in a magical plot to destroy London."

"Rubbish, you knew there was something wrong with the Monument and you thought you could fix it by yourself," I said.

"Doesn't matter," Connie snorted. "He couldn't hear a phone ringing anyway. Not over the sound of how brilliant he is."

Danny rolled his eyes.

"It should have been simple," he said. "Spirits have been talking about someone messing around with the magical energy that feeds the Monument for months. Everyone's been too busy to notice."

"Anyway," I said. "What were you trying to do? London was built as a machine made of streets to hold those creatures, what were you thinking?"

"I thought I had it worked out," Danny said. "I was trying to do a temporary binding until I worked out how to reverse the machine."

Connie tutted. "Because Danny the Sorcerer would never think of such an advanced technique as asking someone. Did you think a normal binding would work? If it was that easy, they wouldn't have built the machine, you idiot!"

"I'm the idiot?" he asked.

Their voices were too much. Their bickering was getting through my ears and into my brain, aggravating everything: from the pain in my hand, to my aching legs, to the cuts all over my arms. I screwed my eyes shut, trying to block them out, but I couldn't move my hand enough to put fingers in both ears.

"Shut it!" I shouted.

There was a moment of silence. In the triangle, the angel made a quiet 'thaw-oth' sound, smoothing its feathers. Connie and Danny looked at each other.

"How could he go out with you for eight weeks without finding out about whatever bizarre condition is affecting your eyes?" I said.

"I didn't like to ask," Danny replied. "It's none of my business. Anyway, are you calling me an idiot?"

Connie touched her glasses. She held them onto her face as tightly as she could.

"No," Connie said. "I'm calling you worse than that."

It was getting harder to think straight and my eyes kept fluttering shut.

"Well," I said, trying not to slur. "That's very nice, but look… we've all explained so much now, Connie… do you just want to tell us who the hell you are? Please? I really want to send all the super-powerful magical beasts away and go to hospital."

"I'm Constance Bloodworth," Connie said. "I'm three hundred and sixty-three years old and my father was Lord Mayor of London during the Great Fire. I stayed alive by making a deal with something in the water and I've been a Master Alchemist for two hundred years."

That's what she said. At least, it's what I think she said. I'll be honest, by the end all I could see was blackness and her voice sounded like it was coming from another universe. I don't know what Danny might have said when she finished, because by then I was drifting somewhere dark, cold and silent.

Chapter Twelve

To be honest I thought that if I woke up at all, I'd be waking up in hospital. I thought there would be daylight, clean sheets and everything would be someone else's problem. I was a bit disappointed when I woke up to find that I was still burnt, soaking wet, dirty and that everything was still on me.

It was dark, too.

On the upside, my hand didn't hurt. I've it said before, a lack of pain is either a very good thing or a very bad thing. In this case I could feel my fingers so it was a fair bet it was a good thing, even if the rest of me still felt like I'd been put in a sack, kicked half to death and dropped in the river. I opened my eyes.

Danny and Connie were standing over me managing not to argue.

"Urgh," I said. "Hi."

Danny looked down at me, then back at Connie. "Alright," he said. "Score one point for alchemy."

"Are you two going to be like this all night?" I asked, trying to get up. "Aren't you supposed to have stopped arguing so that you can unite around getting me back to health?"

"We did," Connie said. "Now you're okay we can start

fighting again."

"I still don't know if I believe you. What did you make a deal with?" I asked.

"I… don't know," Connie shrugged. "I was on a barge leaving the city when it caught fire and overturned. I got tangled up with a burning sail. Imagine that: fire wrapped around you… I fell into the water and got dragged straight to the bottom. Thankfully I knew enough magic to call out for a spirit and I got lucky."

Danny frowned. "But that's like–"

"I know," Connie said. "Dancing on my hands while playing golf with my face, or something like that. Now Esteban is feeling better he can come up with a suitable metaphor. I was desperate and lucky, and you'd be surprised what you can do when you're facing certain death. Unfortunately, it took my eyes."

I nodded. "That's a pretty good metaphor, I might steal it."

Connie huffed, but smiled. Danny chuckled, moving away like happiness was vaguely unsanitary.

"Alright." I pulled myself to my feet. "It's probably a bit obvious, but we've still got the Great Fire to stop."

"That's the bit I think I can help with," Danny said.

"Go on," I said.

Danny pointed to the angel. "Look, I know they tried binding it, hurting it and destroying it, but did anyone ever try talking to it?"

"No," Connie tilted her head. "It doesn't seem very bright. Also, the only thing it seems to do is burn things."

Danny opened his mouth to protest but Connie was in full flow. He stopped and crossed his arms as she continued.

"It murdered people and destroyed a city. It ruined my father's life and cost us a war. It nearly burned me to death, but it might just be *misunderstood?* It isn't as outright evil as the Portent, but it's not on the side of the angels."

"Hang on," Danny put a hand out. "We can try it. If nothing else we might learn something."

"He's got a point, Connie," I said. "What's the worst thing that can happen?"

Connie looked at me as if I'd gone insane. "Well, if you open up communication without the right protection it can possess you, destroy your mind and turn your body into an empty meat puppet."

"We've got to try to talk to it," I said. "I'm sorry Connie, I can't see what else there is to do. We don't really have a choice, do we?"

Connie stared into the circle.

"We might," she said. "But I can't think of anything just now."

Danny shook his dreads loose and re-tied them behind his head.

"Are we all agreed?"

He looked between Connie and me.

"I think all these massive spirits are probably giving me soul cancer," I said rubbing my eyes. "Come on, let's do it."

"Alright, let's give it a try." He looked up at where the bird-angel was fidgeting in the summoning triangle. "Medimiel, could you please bring us the Great Fire?" he asked.

Nothing happened. Danny stood facing Newgate. Fire raged, with the sound of collapsing buildings in the distance. I waited with my heart thudding in my chest. I looked sideways at Danny, who was still looking patiently into the time distortion. I looked at Connie. She was trying to stay cool, shifting from one foot to the other and chewing her knuckles.

We waited in more silence. The angel shuffled around in the circle, preening. It made a soft 'thaw-oth' sound and tucked its head under one wing.

"Dan?" I asked.

"Wait!" he said.

"Dan?" I tried again. "I think–"

"Hush!" Dan put his finger on his lips. "Just wait."

"Dan, I think the Angel's gone to sleep," I said.

Dan just smiled and pointed at the Fire.

A scraping-dragging-crackling noise rumbled through the street, starting quietly, getting louder until it drowned out the sounds of the fire. A chaos of movement and bright, blazing fire meant that we couldn't see what was happening on the other side of Newgate.

"What…?" I looked at Dan and Connie.

Dan just smiled. I realised that the rumbling, moving chaos WAS what was happening. The magical energies around the gate flared and warped as a flaming mass got closer.

I really envied Danny at the centre of his circle. He was the only one of us with any real protection if the Great Fire decided to attack. I looked over to Connie, who was keeping both hands in her pockets.

"So… how much do you actually know about magic, then?" I whispered.

She nodded, "I mastered alchemy and written magic, and some chalk circle work. Unfortunately, I'm almost out of supplies," she said.

"I'd really like to know how long that circle will hold if it tries to destroy Danny," I whispered.

Connie shook her head, "A little longer than the triangle in King Charles' laboratory. On the other hand, Danny's stuck in the circle and we can run away."

I smiled. "Not that I'm planning to," I said. "But I hadn't thought about it like that."

Connie watched the Great Fire advance. She looked ill and worried.

"Every cloud has a silver lining," she said.

The Angel's magic had grabbed the neatly piled rubble from outside Newgate and swept it together into a high column of wood and pitch that led right into Smithfield, past the end of the time distortion. By rights, it should all have disappeared once it was out of the distortion field, but the angel was holding it. This was the power of a conjurer with enough time on their hands: they could summon creatures with the power to do nearly anything.

The Great Fire reached the end of the fuel that had been piled up for it. A face appeared: blunt, with coal-like slit eyes and a gaping mouth. The Great Fire looked around, flaring with emotion when it noticed Connie and me. I saw the angel twitch with the effort of keeping it contained. Danny's circle flared blue-white. He coughed and stumbled back.

"Medimiel," Danny asked. "Can you let us talk to it?"

We both felt the light magical touch as the angel included Connie and me in the spell.

The effect was deafening.

"SEEK. HUNGRY. PAIN. DESTROY," boomed the

Great Fire. "FILTH. PAIN. COLD. HATE IT!"

Its voice was huge. It filled the square. Once I could hear it I could feel my teeth vibrating with every word. Connie and I both clapped our hands over our ears.

"Great Fire, destroyer of cities and bane of Londinium, do you hear us?" Danny asked.

"HATE IT. SEEK IT. BURN IT," the fire bellowed.

"Great Fire," Danny shouted. "By Hermes and Thoth, by Helios and the suns that gave birth to you, by the fires and the salamanders of the earth, do speak with us."

"HATE IT. FIND IT. BURN IT. NICE MEN. SAVE CHILDREN," the Fire raged.

I could see Danny preparing another invocation. It was like trying skeleton keys in a lock: eventually he was going to get the right combination of powers and threats to make it talk, but I wasn't sure we had time.

"You have to stop," I said. "I know they brought you here to stop it, but you're burning the city. You'll kill people."

For a minute I thought I'd made a horrible mistake. Danny almost lost the circle. It flickered when I disrupted his train of thought. The Great Fire looked down and surged. Medimiel twisted and squawked alarmingly. It seemed about to go on without acknowledging us, but something in my voice must have struck a chord. It looked down, as if it was seeing us for the first time (which it probably was, since old, powerful spirits basically see humans as talking ants.)

"Please, we just want to talk to you," I said.

I felt the waves of power coming off it, not just as heat but as pure magical muscle.

It looked down at me.

"SPEAK," it said.

I glanced at Danny. He shrugged. "You've got a minute," Danny said. "It seems to like you."

"Fair enough… look, Great Fire," I said. "You're spreading through the City, twisting time and endangering everyone. If you go on like this there could be really serious damage, not just to the buildings and people, but to time itself. That's why they had to lock you up after 1666."

"REMEMBER," It boomed.

"Good. Look… you've got to stop." I said. "We might be able to sort things."

"PORTENT," the Great Fire Boomed. "STOP IT. CRUSH IT."

"Look, I know," I said. "It's helping the one-eyed man, isn't it?"

"SUMMONED IT. BOUND IT," the Fire said. "SORCERER."

Danny dry retched and dropped to all fours. The turquoise light of his circle flickered out, the angel spread its wings and screeched dangerously. Blue light surged around the Great Fire, holding it back, but only barely.

"That's not much of a surprise," I said, turning to the Great Fire. "What does he want?"

"DOMINION," it boomed.

"Dominion?" Connie asked. "In what way?"

It surged, pouring more and more energy into the conversation. The face twisted like a cave man trying to do calculus. Danny made another pained noise.

"Look," Danny gasped. "I can't keep this up much

longer."

I looked up to the Great Fire. "Look, please, tell us straight: what should we do?"

"THE ONE-EYED MAN BROUGHT IT TO KILL AND CAUSE PAIN. THE ONE-EYED MAN BRINGS WAR, PLAGUE. MISERY IS HIS JOY," explained the Great Fire.

"THAT IS WHY I CHASE IT. IT HATES. IT KILLS."

That was when I realised that the Great Fire wasn't stupid, it was careful. It had only been using as much power as Danny could handle. Its voice hit like a tidal wave. I felt the sickening pain of the angel's spell lashing back straight through Danny, who had collapsed, his circle turning dark.

The blue aura that had contained it blinked out. The fire rushed at us. Flame burst out in every direction. Medimiel streaked towards Danny, throwing him clear of the attack.

Connie screamed in blind fear and clawed her dark glasses off.

It was one of the most wrong things I've ever seen: the skin around her eyes was glistening, black and wet. Where her eyes should have been there were just hollows full of white light.

She spread her arms wide and stared the Great Fire down, fixing those empty eye sockets on it. The two bright pinpoints flared.

"Back!" she snarled.

I felt something huge work through her. Less than 200 metres away the Fleet river tried to break through twenty feet of concrete. The river Thames rose up and crashed down onto the city.

Danny looked over at his angel. My second lesson of the night was how fast Danny could get through the long-winded language of conjuration. His lips fluttered without missing a syllable. His words reigned the angel in, sharpening its attention. It probably took about ten seconds from start to finish.

By the end he was shouting. "…Angel of words, angel of works. You who taught writing to the infancy of man, send the fire back. Send it back!"

Medimiel shrieked and disappeared. The Great Fire hissed like it had been doused with water. All over the city, water mains burst and sprinklers started spouting. The modern City of London tried to coexist with 1666 and won out, spilling water all over the airless fires of Restoration London. Steam and choking smoke rose up from the burning timbers.

The time bubble warped and collapsed as the zones fought for dominance. The tension between the Great Fire's time distortion and the city defences broke, snapping out a wave of temporal shock that made me sick to my stomach with the Devil's ringtone chiming in my ears.

Chapter Thirteen

I was cold and soaked to the skin. Again. Wet tarmac glistened beetle black in the streetlights. A chorus of car alarms and burglar alarms shrieked as the freak waves obediently receded into the waters, having smashed down on the city.

Time still wasn't right: modern buildings stood next to ones from 1666. Smoke curled up into the sky, but it wasn't raining birds. There was a glow of fire, but it wasn't bright enough to turn night into day.

Danny had been dragged a few feet out of his circle, still face down. I stumbled over to him. Steam rose off all three of us. After the unbearable heat of the fire, the chill of the night made me shiver.

"Dan?" I asked. "Are you alright? Dan?"

I stopped at the edge of the circle. I didn't want to cross the line unless I had to. It was probably dead now, but you never knew what kind of magical energies were still kicking around.

"Danny?" I called again. "Can you hear me? Da–"

"I can hear you, mate," he said, not moving. "That was interesting. Don't do it again."

Connie was standing stiff as a post, arms at her sides, dark glasses back on. Her face was as expressionless as a shop dummy.

"Umm…" I said. "Yeah, probably best if I don't. Can you move?"

A cloud passed over Danny's face. "I had a go at binding it," he said.

Cold horror settled over me.

"How did that go for you?" I asked.

Danny peered out at the still-burning streets. "I managed to pull it back a bit," he said. "You might notice the angel isn't here anymore."

"Yeah," I said. "Are you going to pay for that?"

Danny shrugged. "He's an angel, they're supposed to be forgiving…"

A line of suppressed worry appeared on Danny's forehead but I pretended not to see it. He looked around, playing with one of his dreadlocks as he thought through what had just happened.

It was then that I went back to Connie.

"I might have lost my temper a bit," she mumbled. "Sorry about that."

"You know," said Danny looking at her. "The answer to a horrible disaster threatening to destroy the city is NOT to replace it with a different disaster."

Connie gave him a murderous look.

"Said the Chalk-Circle Man?" she hissed.

"Alright," I stepped between them. "Connie, what was that?"

"I don't know," she held her glasses onto her face. "It was the thing that took my eyes. I've had a feeling it's been watching us. I wasn't really in control for a while. It just took control and did what it needed."

"Right, well if you get anymore feelings about it, can

you tell us?" I asked.

Connie nodded unwillingly. "Alright."

She shook herself. "We might be slightly better off than we were an hour ago." She looked at Danny. "I'm glad we found you."

Danny looked at Connie and smiled a quiet, smirking grin.

"Anyway, look," I said. "This is all the one-eyed man. He just seems to get off on wrecking things, and we've got to stop him."

"That's true," Danny said. "Just restart the machine before it goes wrong. That would reset everything. I could do the ritual parts, you could do the alchemy."

"Hang on," I said. "Will this mean me taking the whole city back in time?"

"Not for long," Connie said. "Just a couple of minutes."

"Yeah," Danny said. "And it's not Greater London, just the Square Mile."

I shook my head. The hope in their faces was like a punch in the stomach.

"I can't do it. I've already pushed myself to my limit."

Danny clapped a hand on my shoulder.

"I know mate," he said. "But it can't get any worse, can it? We've got to try something."

I shook my head again.

"Now I know why you two are together. You're both insane."

"That's the spirit." Connie grinned. "For now, we've got to get moving. We probably haven't got much time before it tries to kill us again."

Something moved in the shadows. Several somethings.

I heard The Devil's ringtone, the tinkling sound of magical energy, drifting on the night air.

"Umm…" I said. "Maybe even less time than we thought."

I thought I saw something move in the shadows again.

"What was that?" I looked around.

Something giggled in the darkness: a quiet noise, but too close for comfort. If I hadn't been looking at her, I would have thought it had come from Connie. I spun around, but there was nothing there.

"I think we've got company," I said.

"The Monument held the Great Fire, but it wasn't the whole machine," Danny explained. "Christopher Wren proposed a whole circuit made of streets, buildings and churches here in the City of London. Two thousand cubits by two thousand cubits, with the Temple Church and St. Paul's as the control centre and mechanism."

"What does the rest of it hold?" I asked.

"Think about it, Esteban," Danny said. "Why do you think London doesn't have any monsters: dark faeries, devil pigs, or things that go bump in the night? Have you ever been to Paris or Berlin? Why do you think the only predators here are muggers?"

"But there used to be lots," Connie said. "There were once, just not any more."

"Okay," I asked cautiously. "What's going on?"

"London didn't have any monsters," Danny said. "Past tense. Now the machine isn't working."

Skittering in the darkness, glowing points of lights winked on, first one, then another.

"What are those things?" said Danny.

He stepped back, looking for his discarded hat and

backpack.

More eyes: four pairs, then eight.

"Link Folk," Connie said. "There were no street lights, so kids used to make money carrying lamps and torches for rich people. After the fire, these things moved in and started eating people."

Sixteen pairs. Probably. I stopped counting when it got to a lot. There were definitely more of them than there were of us.

"So they're ghosts?" Danny asked.

We stood back to back.

"They're cowards," Connie said. "They lead people into dark, lonely places and attack them. What have we got?"

Danny shook his head. "I've got nothing," he said. "I need time."

"This isn't fair," Connie said. "Time is supposed to be flowing normally. This would never happen in the daylight."

The Link Folk whispered in the shadows. Voices curled around in the darkness. It sounded like there were a lot more of them than we could see. Their whispering and chattering filled the air.

"I've had enough of this," I shouted. "You lot! I don't suppose you happened to notice when we summoned an unknown spirit, a fire god and an angel?"

I looked at the flickering shadows, the creatures laughed.

I grabbed a minute of daylight.

White light shone through Smithfield, flooding out the black and orange night. For half a second I got the impression of grey, shrieking imps.

They ran away a lot less gracefully than they'd snuck up on us: screaming, falling over each other and knocking over bins. I listened to the sounds of running footsteps until I was sure they'd all gone.

Day turned back into night. I blinked heavily.

"Are we going to have a lot more of that?" I moaned, squinting into the darkness.

"Maybe," Danny said. "With any luck word'll get out that we're not worth crossing."

Connie tapped her lips.

"Just like the old days."

"Right," I said. "Connie? Remember that map we got at massive risk to our lives? The one that has all that magical notation that you and Danny can decipher?"

"Yes," Connie winced. "But we've been soaked and burned a few times since then though."

She took out the folded square of paper. It was a single stained soggy lump.

Danny untied and retied his dreads, frowning thoughtfully.

"We need the plans. Not just a map of London, we need to work out how they built the magical effect. There must be particular shapes and patterns of streets that make it work. If I could get a look at that map, I could probably find a ritual that would make the city work again."

"And then would it start sucking up monsters again?" I asked

"That's how it worked before." Connie adjusted her shades. "It absorbed them into the stones of the city. But we would need the plans. I should have put them somewhere safer."

"It's okay," I said. "Where in London did Robert Hook and Christopher Wren do all their best scientific work? Where did they set up a temporary Royal Exchange so that trade could continue even after the Great Fire?"

Connie's face lit up. I saw a tiny flicker of light behind her shades.

"Gresham College," she grinned. "Even if the plans, or a copy, ended up in the lab, they must have been at Gresham College while they were designing the city."

"We'd better move then," said Danny picking up his bag. "If I was the one-eyed man, I'd be there right now torching anything that someone could use to stop me."

Connie ran, haring off around the corner. I ignored the fact that I was exhausted and aching all over, and started jogging after her.

Danny watched us run. He walked to the bike rack. The only thing left on it was a black mountain bike.

"No planning," said Danny unlocking the bike and throwing the chain around his neck. "Am I the only one who thinks of these things?"

Chapter Fourteen

"Are you sure the plans will be here?" Connie gasped.

"Not really," I leaned against a lamp post. "But they were here at some point in time, and that means we can get a look at them."

Even Connie had lost her breath after the long run from Smithfield to Bishopsgate. Time was still a jumble, even here. Bits of Gresham college were still coexisting with the present, but most of it had returned to the past. Annoyingly, the half that was still here wasn't the half we needed. The other half was a tall glass skyscraper, trying to coexist with the 17th century mansion.

Thankfully, it was a magical space, like Middle Thames Street.

Danny cycled effortlessly past, looking for doors with the strongest hint of the past. He got off and propped his bike against a closed chicken shop, walking up and down the street with an incense stick.

"Here," he waved us over. "Around the corner."

Every London backstreet is a little bit temporally unfocussed. There's just so much time weighing down on the city. The glass gave way to stone wall; the pavement was flagstone with a groove for the rainwater. Danny touched a metal-studded door with a heavy iron grill.

"Yeah…" he said. "This is it."

"Is it from the past… or has someone just left it here for a long time?" asked Connie as she peered through the grill.

"I don't know," I said. "If I can trigger the doorway it'll transport us to Gresham Collage, or at least a recreation of it."

I reached out and pushed. Daylight streamed in. We were standing in a sunlit colonnade around a square garden. People were setting up stalls and directing apprentices to bring in reams of paper and barrels of goods. Men in frock coats with unrealistically curly hair directed less well dressed men, probably clerks, in how to arrange their desks.

"These aren't real people, are they?" Connie asked, looking at the clerks running around.

"Probably not," I said. "Even if they were, being stuck in a 'trap' street for hundreds of years, repeating the same series of actions probably hasn't done anything good for them."

"Alright…" said Danny looking around. "Christopher Wren's office… the question is, which one is it? We could ask someone, but I don't think these are spirits. It would go against the usual construction of a trap street. They'd collapse the structure."

"If you say so," I said. "We might still be able to get directions."

Connie coughed politely as a man in a brown curly wig came past.

"Your pardon?" she asked. "Could you direct me to Master Wren's rooms?"

The young man turned. He had a faded, unreal quality. The white makeup and painted-on rosy cheeks didn't help.

"What…the…?" Danny whispered.

The young man either didn't notice or couldn't hear us.

"On the other side of the quad Miss, just follow the other gentleman," he said.

I had a sinking feeling.

"Was it a man with one eye?" I asked.

The brown haired man nodded and drifted off.

"We haven't seen him for ages," Connie kicked something. "Blooded Nails. We've been running around getting half killed and he's probably got the plans."

We ran, shoving through the shades. There were rooms on the other side of the quad, each with a brass plaque bearing a name. Straight ahead there was one with the name 'Christopher Wren.' It was open.

I looked at Connie and Danny.

"Give me your hands," I said.

They took a hand each and I heaved them into the past. It wasn't easy, but this was an unreal place and time was fluid enough to manipulate.

People flickered past and shadows shortened. The artificial sun went backwards through the sky. A figure shot through the door but we couldn't see him. I went back as far as I could. When we searched Wren's rooms, I wanted to do it undisturbed.

Time solidified again, this time with strange soft edges as I held the past in place.

"Minutes," I said. "We've got minutes. Come on!"

The only problem was that in all the excitement, I'd

forgotten that the door would be closed and locked.

Connie read my expression and laughed.

"Don't worry," she said as she searched through her pockets. "I've got something."

It was the same green bottle she'd used on the bear. Connie unscrewed the top and poured a few drops into the lock, which fizzed and smoked.

"Here we go," she said, pushing the door.

Bits of the lock fell out, melting from the powerful acid. We went in, with Danny and Connie taking the lead.

"Okay, be quick," I said. "I can't hold us in the past for very long."

There were bookshelves full of old books. All the furniture looked authentic and there were yards of velvet everywhere, not to mention the clockwork machines.

Danny looked at the bookshelves. Suspicious shapes poked out from behind the books.

"Have we got time to search all this?" he asked.

"No chance," I said, barely pushing the words out. "We won't be here that long."

"Alright mate?" said Danny, putting a hand on my shoulder. "Hold on as long as you can."

I nodded.

"Where would you put the plans? Assuming you know something was up?" Danny asked, looking under some ancient pieces of paper.

"They did know," said Connie as she opened every drawer in the desk. "They probably knew more than we do."

There were too many places: doors into two other rooms, cabinets stuffed full of papers, and years worth of nick nacks. Even if we stuck to the main room it would still take hours.

Time flickered. We saw a still image, a split-second as the one-eyed man tried to see through time. He was looking at something on the side wall.

"What was that?" said Connie.

She walked over to where he'd been standing.

"I lost my grip for a second. Sorry," I said.

There was no way I was going to be able to move the whole city.

"Good," Connie said. "Do it again."

Danny paused from taking books off the shelves. "There's a lot of stuff back here… nothing magical," he said.

Time slipped again. The one-eyed man was kneeling, clawing at the carpet. He looked towards us and disappeared. Time wriggled twice as hard, desperately trying to get free and throw us back into the present.

"He's coming through," I said.

"It's alright," Connie gasped. "Danny, help me."

A fresh paradox wave nearly shook my grip loose. Admittedly, that wasn't hard. You could have popped a balloon next to me and done the same thing. The one-eyed man moved through time.

"He's coming," I said. "Quick!"

Danny shoved a table back and pulled the carpet away from the floor to reveal a small door. There was a click as he opened it.

The machine that rose out of the floor was beautiful: brass and mahogany with a glass cylinder full of thick, black liquid. Gears and counterweights whirled like an ornate clock.

The one-eyed man was close, he crackled with the Portent's decaying energy.

"I can't stop him." I said. "He's taken power from the Portent."

The machine opened like a flower, blossoming to reveal a silver bowl on a purple velvet cushion. A scrolled piece of paper rose out of the centre. Danny breathed a sigh of relief and snatched it up.

"No! Danny… sto–"

Connie lunged forward.

The machine chimed. All around the glass cylinder, silver-plated hammers arched back with a click.

"Go!" Connie shouted.

The one-eyed man appeared, his face twisted into a mask of rage.

I let go of my spell.

Four silver plated hammers snapped forward and shattered the glass cylinder. Black ooze touched the air and exploded into fire.

The one-eyed man covered his face with his arms. We snapped back to the present. Fire flashed out over the entire room in a split second.

The one-eyed man howled and tried to hold me in the past. There are probably several techniques for inter-temporal duelling, but I've never known any of them. I just kicked back, jarring his hold on the time stream. He swore in three languages. I stuttered back and forth in time until he couldn't hold me anymore.

We appeared in the cold, sooty shell of Wren's living room. One of the wooden doors was off its hinges, revealing a bedroom full of dark wood and red velvet.

"Are we okay?" Danny asked.

"I–" I started.

The one-eyed man appeared, and grabbed me by the throat. Time lurched backwards again. I could feel the time-stopped fire waiting to burn me up, if I wasn't torn apart by the explosion.

I twisted. He snarled, redoubling his grip.

"What do you want?" I twisted around. "What good is this doing you?"

His good eye was bright, mad and feverish. He had sharp teeth like the Portent. He giggled.

"London," he said. "I get London sealed up in a bubble of captive time. Mine forever."

I was at my limit. He was stronger, and had more power in the timestream. He almost dragged me back and I could feel the heat dying in reverse as I got closer to the explosion.

I kicked at his shins. It wasn't high magic, or even low magic. His face distorted with pain as I kicked him again, as hard as I could.

The one-eyed man dropped back into the past. I reappeared with the soles of my shoes smoking.

"Come on, let's go," I said. "He didn't feel human anymore. Don't think there's much difference between him and the Portent now."

"Won't he come back to the present?" said Danny as he looked around.

"No. I project through time, but he's really time travelling. Demons and spirits can do that. And my grandmother," I replied.

I shook my head. This wasn't in my league. "Whatever the Portent is, it's given him the same ability."

It was at about that point that I noticed Connie hadn't

spoken for a while.

She was standing in the middle of the room, gripping her bag so hard that her fingers were white. She stared straight forward. Her dark glasses meant that I couldn't work out whether she was afraid or angry.

"Connie?" I asked carefully.

Danny went very quiet and circled around behind her. If she noticed she didn't show it.

"Connie, are you alright?" I touched her shoulder.

Her hand snapped up as fast as lightning, grabbing mine and crushing my knuckles together painfully. She twisted my hand through 180 degrees and shouted into my face.

"No more fire!" she screamed. "No more fire or burning. I can't take it."

She twisted my hand until I cried out. "No more fire. I can't it. I'll kill you if there's anymore fire, do you hear? I'll… kill… you…"

"Connie!" Danny tried to prize her hands off me.

"Get off me!" cried Connie shoving him out of the way, still shaking me. "No more fire." Tears rolled down her cheeks. "No more!"

"No more fire," I said. "No more fire at all, I promise. You've made it this far. You can do it."

Connie took a shuddering breath and burst into tears. I let her cry on my shoulder, putting an arm around her.

"I'm sorry," she whispered, after a while. "But I really will kill you if there's any more fire. Well, not kill. Just injure you, probably."

I didn't say anything. I wondered if Danny might have something to say about Connie crying on my shoulder rather than his.

"Guys," Danny said. "We really don't have time."

He opened what was left of the door back into the quad. "We need to get out of here before our friend comes back."

"Wait," said Connie. "Do we have the map?"

Danny held up the scroll.

"It looks like it."

He took off the ribbon and opened it.

"Yeah." His eyes flickered over it. "This is it."

Then I heard it: the music I'd been hearing all my life. The Devil's ringtone.

"Can you hear that?" said Danny raising an eyebrow.

"You can hear it too?" I asked.

Connie wiped her face and frowned. "That's really, really annoying," she said.

"That's the Devil's ringtone," I said. "I always hear it, whenever there's magic around. I've been hearing it nearly all day."

"We've been doing a lot of time stuff today," I said. "You've probably just got a bit of me in your heads."

"Does that mean we can help you when we try to kick start the machine?" said Danny frowning.

I could see the wheels turning in his head.

"I don't know, can you?" I shrugged. "You're the technical one."

Danny nodded. "Maybe."

"Then let's go. That sound probably means the one-eyed man is coming back."

Chapter Fifteen

Once we got out into the street we realised we didn't have long: flakes of snow were twisting through the air, battling with the cinders that fluttered on the burning breeze. The heat still made me sweat, but the air between gusts from the fire was freezing cold. Snow clouds and ash clouds battled for dominance, flickering lights rippling through the sky.

My grandmother was sealing off the city.

Danny was deadly quiet as we hurried from Bishopsgate over to St. Paul's Cathedral. He's a good friend, but I've never really understood what goes on in his head. Connie walked in front of us, looking around like a caged animal. Danny slowed down, letting her get even further ahead.

"Are you okay?" I asked quietly.

Danny didn't answer, walking with his eyes fixed on the road, concentrating on putting one foot in front of another.

"I wouldn't have cared about Connie messing with the Great Fire," he said eventually.

"She claims she didn't mess with it," I said.

"Why else would Connie hide who she is?" he asked.

Connie looked back, overhearing our conversation.

"I'm hundreds of years old. My whole life is a lie. I'm sorry, I just freaked out. Even magical people do that sometimes," she said.

Danny went quiet again. We'd reached the top of the rise before St. Paul's. The green light was close enough that we could see it splashing through the streets, bleaching out the glow of the fire. Even the buildings had turned green, with tiny pools of normal light where they were burning. The weather was trying to be two things at once: hot and ice cold at the same time.

The modern buildings rose up out of the slightly transparent buildings of 1666, which were still on fire. St. Paul's was ancient and modern at the same time: a crumbling gothic spire rose out of the modern cathedral's dome. Flurries of snow fell and melted in mid air. Burning pieces of paper fluttered on the breeze.

"It's nearly done. I've got an idea for the ritual," Danny said, frowning. "It'll take about half an hour. Have we got long enough?"

"Probably, yeah," I replied, faking confidence. "No trouble."

Danny opened the map and glared at it.

"I think..." Danny stopped walking.

He looped his arm around Connie's shoulders. She tensed up for a second, but she let him.

"Here's how I think it works," he said. "This is the actual control mechanism, which Connie will need to set with an alchemical tincture. The ritual can only be effective at one point in all of time – Esteban, that's your job – I just need to get to the right part of the ritual, and tip you the wink so you won't have to hold us for the whole thing."

"What kind of tincture?" Connie asked.

"The Alessandro preparation," Danny said.

Connie chewed her lip. "I've got the stuff," she said. "But I'm going to need an open flame."

She laughed. "Wonderful, more flame."

"It's alright, there's a cafe in the shopping centre," Danny said. "There'll be a cooker in the kitchen."

"I can probably mix and prepare it in about fifteen minutes," said Connie.

Danny smiled. It was one of the least annoying smiles I'd ever seen on him.

"I like your spirit," he said.

I smiled too. I put my hands in my pocket so that they couldn't see me shaking. We were coming to where the Ludgate hill curved down towards Farringdon road. I could make out my grandmother standing in the middle of the road.

I turned to the others.

"Go," I said. "I'll try and keep her talking."

Abuela looked tired. I'd assumed that Connie and I had the monopoly on being tired, injured and frightened, but she looked worse. She stood in the middle of the road, every inch of her was trembling from the effort. She was bolt upright. Donna Caterina Cova Callas wasn't going to do what needed doing while shivering on her knees.

"A-Abuela…" I said.

She looked down at me, her face a stern mask of concentration.

"Abuela?" I said again, eying her suspiciously.

"Your clothes are a mess," she replied. "You look like you've been rolling in mud, soot and razor-blades. It's a disgusting thing to do to a helpless old woman at the end of her life."

"I-I'm sorry," I looked around for any sign of the one-eyed man. "Is he here?"

She shook her head.

"No, but he's so strong…" she reached out for me but pulled her hand back. "He's almost one with the creature now."

"What does it want?" I whispered.

"Power and pain," she said. "It loves power and pain."

"Can you help us?" I asked.

"I've been fighting him all night," said Abuela shaking her head. "I have to seal the city. It's almost too late now. I barely have the strength."

"But you might make things worse…" I moaned.

"I can see no other option," Abuela said. "Better to seal them here in a dominion of two than have an immortal sorcerer and an evil spirit engineer human suffering."

I glanced back at Connie and Danny. Connie vanished into the shopping centre and Danny went the other way, into the Cathedral.

"Abuela…" I said grabbing her coat. "Please don't do this. We've nearly got it sorted."

Something moved in the shadows.

"Please," I said. "I'm going to try and move the city. We've got the plans for the magical machine they were using to hold the spirits in place the first time. We can start it all up again."

My grandmother sighed and shook her head. She gave me a look of genuine pity.

"Esteban–" she started.

I had time to hear the Devil's ringtone before St. Paul's Cathedral came to life. Energy raced out from the cathedral to the Wren church on Ludgate Hill, down to St. Brides, across to St. Mary Woolnoth and on to the Guildhall and Paternoster Square.

"Please?" I looked into her eyes. This wasn't going to work, she never changed her mind. "What difference will it make if you do it now or in five minutes?"

My grandmother looked over at the cathedral. I was shouting over the Devil's ringtone. Between it and the thundering of magical energy I could barely hear myself. I could feel the vibrations of Danny's ritual rippling out. A false dawn leapt up over London as magical power came flaring up from under the streets.

My grandmother looked past me. Cannon Street was a river of white light.

"That's how they imprisoned the Portent last time, and the Great Fire." I said pointing at the cathedral. "That's why London doesn't have any goblins and things that go bump in the night. Christopher Wren and Robert Hook redesigned the city. They rebuilt it and they hid a magical circuit in the streets. St. Paul's is the control centre. The Monument was the focal point of the energy. We can reset everything. We can stuff them all back inside."

"I–" my grandmother started. "Hostia! You spend too much time with that boy."

She was smiling. I smiled back. "Will you help me? This will either fail or succeed really quickly. You'll know soon enough, either way."

"You're a fool," she said smiling. "It probably runs in the family."

Chapter Sixteen

My grandmother nodded, and we pulled at time. The landscape blurred and dim red mist crept around the edges of my vision. Modern buildings slipped in and out of focus as I tried to drag Connie, Danny, myself and the whole of Christopher Wren's masterpiece into the early hours of the morning on one particular day of the 17th century.

My grandmother is the Archmage of Chronomancy. That means she's officially the most powerful Chronomancer around, for now. The problem is, pulling a truck with someone really strong is still pulling a truck. It hurts. I was starting to wonder what would be left of me after this.

A heard a strange echo of Danny's voice and the cathedral's main doors popped open. His part of the ritual had worked: he virtually WAS the building.

I ran up the steps, barely holding onto the effect, even with my grandmother helping me. I could feel how tired she was now.

I ran into the cathedral. Connie had come through a door on the other side. At the centre of the cathedral the brass floor decoration was glowing with an ornate magical circle. Danny stood at the centre with a wand in one hand and a sword in the other. An aluminium bowl was on the floor just in front of him.

His eyes glowed. A pulsing beam of energy came down from the centre of the dome into the tip of his sword. That's the thing with conjurers: they can do amazing things with magic, but they need to be left alone to do it.

Danny touched the space above the edge of the circle. The air vibrated.

"Come and help me in the circle," he said, waving me in. "Connie, you too. We need you to put the tincture into the bowl in the middle of the circle."

There was a sickening surge of energy. It was almost strong enough to put me off. Even Danny stammered over his incantation. The one-eyed man appeared between us and Connie. His face was dark with anger. I stepped over the circle to stand next to Danny. My mind was whirring. He could hurt Connie. If he pushed, he might even be able to get through Danny's circle.

"I really don't understand you," I said. "How long have you been scheming and hurting people just to get a reaction?"

"Chronomancers," the one-eyed man sneered. "Never letting the past stay buried."

Connie was still moving. She slipped her shoes off, stepping silently towards the circle, making a wide arc behind the one-eyed man. My heart tried to jackhammer its way out of my chest.

"Why are you doing all this?" I asked. "Whatever you want, there are easier ways to get it."

The one-eyed man laughed bitterly. The Portent's energy didn't just crackle through him, it was him. He took the patch off his eye, revealing a goat's eye like the one in its chest. He smiled with a mouth full of sharp, misshapen teeth.

"We will live forever, and this will be our domain," he said. "We will be the emperor of everything that remains."

"Is that it?" I asked, watching Connie edge around to the triangle. "You actually want the city to be sealed?"

The one-eyed man snarled. "I want a domain to rule. I have chosen this one."

I tried not to watch Connie creeping around behind it.

"So, what? You'd rather be in charge, even in prison? Why?" I asked.

"We have lived this long, but not much longer," he replied.

The one-eyed man shook his head. "All have surpassed us by nothing more than fortune and accidents of birth. We will rule here for eternity."

Connie put her head down and sprinted towards us. The one-eyed man's personality melted away as the Portent hissed with a thousand voices. Even his body suddenly seemed empty and hollow – a puppet worked by something horrible. If there was anything left of him, I didn't want to think about it.

It lashed out with deathly cold. The cathedral's marble floor cracked as it dropped to hundreds of degrees below zero.

Connie screamed as her feet touched the ground. She fell, supporting herself with one hand and yelped as she stumbled forward. Danny bled from his fingertips as he tried to maintain the circle, his lips moving quickly over the strange magical formula. Connie wailed and swore in Restoration English. I reached out to drag her into the circle.

"No," Danny hissed. "She's got to get here by herself. Keep your time effect stable or we'll break the circle."

The Portent grinned at us and threw another blast of deadly cold at Connie. She stumbled, losing the skin on her hand when she touched the floor. I strained to keep the time effect going.

"The grandmother, the pet conjurer," the Portent's voice was like a swarm of bees. "Humans, all of you. You supplanted us. Replaced us. How dare you!"

Shards of ice smacked against the marble, almost knocking Connie off her feet. He threw a volley of them at us. They shattered in the air above the circle. Danny shuddered. I could feel the whole thing slipping away.

The Portent laughed, "I am disease, I am destruction. I am the final death and decay of everything. I am the utter cold when every corpse has cooled and every sun has died."

I grabbed hold of time extra hard and concentrated on keeping us in the moment. Connie was almost at the edge of the circle.

I stepped to the side so that she could come in. My face hurt. I couldn't tell whether I was baring my teeth or smiling.

The Portent took two strides forward and grabbed her by the hair. I could see the fear on Danny's face, but he didn't stop muttering the spell.

"You–" Connie struggled to throw a bottle over its shoulder. The tincture.

The Portent laughed and batted the bottle away, grabbing her wrist.

"Blood winged son of a..." Connie shouted.

There was a snap-crunch as the Portent broke her arm.

Connie didn't scream this time. Her whole body shivered, but she didn't make a sound. The Portent snarled and threw aside her dark glasses. Connie screwed her eyes shut.

"Danny!" I said.

"No," he said. "Keep doing your part."

The Portent fixed her with its goat eye. Even in the circle, I could feel its malevolent power.

"I will freeze your spirit and shatter it," the Portent said. "And then I then I shall really start hurting you. Look into my eyes."

Connie tried to turn her head, but the demon yanked her by the hair so that she had to face it.

"Open your eyes," it said. "Open them or I will step over the circle and hurt your friends."

Connie tensed.

"Open them!" it said.

Connie opened her eyes. Hollow pits with glowing points of light looked out.

The Portent gasped.

"Don't you like what you see?" Connie laughed. "Look at it. I don't even know what it is, but it's huge, and it hates you."

The Portent grunted and looked away. It shook itself and doubled its grip on Connie. Her laughter died on her lips.

"No," it said. "It cannot venture here. Not now you

have activated the machine."

Connie flailed and twisted. The Portent laughed and jerked her a little higher into the air.

"Yes," it said. "I think I will destroy you. Then I shall step into the circle and finish off your friends."

"Bloodied Nails!" said Connie, gritting her teeth.

She arched her back and stretched her leg out. She managed to catch the fallen bottle with her toe and flick it into the circle. The Portent screamed, howled and hissed in a dozen voices at once.

I snatched up the bottle and poured the electric blue fluid into the bowl.

Danny opened his eyes. "That's it," he said. "We're finished."

The Devil's ringtone sounded loud and clear, making the Cathedral dome chime. The Portent tried to throw Connie, sending her rolling across the floor. She thumped into one of the pews.

A triangle appeared around the Portent. It howled.

The alchemical tincture hissed and bubbled away.

"Double, double, toil and trouble," Danny muttered. "Fire burn and cauldron bubble."

A pulse of light flashed along the line of power between the Cathedral and the Monument. Fire and explosive damage repaired itself. The Monument blossomed back into full repair like a strange flower.

Link Folk, dark faeries, goblins, faceless men and night time horrors melted into the pavement. Streets rearranged themselves. In the morning people would blame the roadworks and remember nothing. London had reset itself.

The Portent vanished. What was left of the one-eyed

man dropped to the floor.

The cathedral settled back into shape with a peal of bells. The effect snapped back so hard that Danny and I went flying in opposite directions. I slid across the marble floor, coming to a halt much more gently than Connie had. We lay in silence for a while.

"Is he dead?" Danny said, eventually.

"Well... he's completely flat and his eyes have melted, so I hope so," I said. "I can get up and poke him with a stick, if you like?"

"Yeah," said Danny. "I think my sword is around here somewhere."

"Is it sharp, by the way?"

"Nah," he said. "It's just ceremonial."

The air was warm, but not sweltering. A cool, but not icy, breeze came in through the open door.

"Did it work?" I asked.

"Does it feel like your grandmother is trying to seal the city off?" Danny asked.

"No," I replied.

I tried to get up and slumped back onto the floor. "It feels like everything's back to normal. Except my body. My body feels like I've been walked on." Outside people were shouting.

"Okay," I said as I looked over at Danny. "Paper, rock, scissors to see who gets up and finds Connie some medical attention?"

In the end it turned out that St. Paul's Cathedral had a cupboard full of wheelchairs. We put Connie in one, but she was like a rag doll. She slumped in the wheelchair, looking almost boneless, as we wheeled her down the ramp. Personally, I found my injuries were wearing off quickly now that the city wasn't being menaced by demons.

Confused police officers were starting to arrive. Some very odd reports had probably started coming in. A helicopter chopped away up in the night sky.

My grandmother looked between us, still smiling.

"It's late again," she said. "And I shouldn't be up so late, not at my time of life… but I have something in the fridge if any of you don't feel like sleeping?"

My stomach growled. The rest of me would probably start hurting at some point, but right now my stomach was reminding me that I hadn't really had anything to eat in 24 hours.

"What are we going to do with Connie?" I said, nodding at her. "She can't look after herself."

"She can come back with us," Abuela said. "Just this once. And so can Danny, if he's not expected anywhere."

"Thanks…" said Danny, shuffling his feet. "But I'm probably going to take Connie somewhere to get healed. It might be complicated, considering she's hundreds of years old."

"Okay," I said. "But don't be a stranger, alright?"

Connie moaned, stirring in her chair. "Esteban," she said. "We're only going to hospital, so get that look off your face." She looked at my grandmother. "I don't think we can accept your invitation. Please don't feel there's any disrespect."

My grandmother smiled and bobbed her head. "Never," she said.

Danny looked around. "And I think we can all agree that we've made an enemy tonight."

"Maybe, yeah," I said. "But at least life will never get boring."

By Robin Price & Paul McGrory

Jemima Mallard's year has not started well. First she loses her air, then someone steals her houseboat, and now the Youth Cops think she's mixed up with a criminal called Father Thames. Not even her dad, a Chief Inspector with the 'Dult Police, can help her out this time. Oh – and London's still sinking. It's been underwater ever since the climate upgrade. All in all, it's looking like deep trouble for the girl they call 'Miss Hap'.
The story is told in words and over 70 stunning illustrations.

ISBN: 978-1-906132-03-3
UK £7.99
USA $14.95 / CAN $16.95

Get a sneak peak at some illustrations from London Deep by visiting www.mogzilla.co.uk